Science Fiction: A Very Short Introduction

VERY SHORT INTRODUCTIONS are for anyone wanting a stimulating and accessible way in to a new subject. They are written by experts, and have been published in more than 25 languages worldwide.

The series began in 1995, and now represents a wide variety of topics in history, philosophy, religion, science, and the humanities. The VSI Library now contains over 200 volumes—a Very Short Introduction to everything from ancient Egypt and Indian philosophy to conceptual art and cosmology—and will continue to grow to a library of around 300 titles.

Very Short Introductions available now:

Available soon:

For more information visit our website

www.oup.com/vsi/

David Seed

SCIENCE FICTION

A Very Short Introduction

OXFORD
UNIVERSITY PRESS

OXFORD

UNIVERSITY PRESS

Great Clarendon Street, Oxford ox2 6dp

Oxford University Press is a department of the University of Oxford.
It furthers the University's objective of excellence in research, scholarship,
and education by publishing worldwide in

Oxford New York

Auckland Cape Town Dar es Salaam Hong Kong Karachi
Kuala Lumpur Madrid Melbourne Mexico City Nairobi
New Delhi Shanghai Taipei Toronto

With offices in

Argentina Austria Brazil Chile Czech Republic France Greece
Guatemala Hungary Italy Japan Poland Portugal Singapore
South Korea Switzerland Thailand Turkey Ukraine Vietnam

Oxford is a registered trade mark of Oxford University Press
in the UK and in certain other countries

Published in the United States
by Oxford University Press Inc., New York

© David Seed 2011

The moral rights of the author have been asserted
Database right Oxford University Press (maker)

First published 2011

British Library Cataloguing in Publication Data

Data available

Library of Congress Cataloging in Publication Data

Data available

Typeset by SPI Publisher Services, Pondicherry, India
Printed in Great Britain
on acid-free paper by
Ashford Colour Press Ltd, Gosport, Hampshire

ISBN 978–0–19–955745–5

1 3 5 7 9 10 8 6 4 2

Contents

List of illustrations

The publisher and the author apologise for any errors or omissions in the above list. If contacted they will be happy to rectify these at the earliest opportunity.

Science Fiction

Introduction

Science fiction has proved notoriously difficult to define. It has variously been explained as a combination of romance, science, and prophecy (Hugo Gernsback), 'realistic speculation about future events' (Robert Heinlein), and a genre based on an imagined alternative to the reader's environment (Darko Suvin). It has been called a form of fantastic fiction and an historical literature. This volume will not attempt to reduce these explanations to a single, comprehensive definition. That way madness lies. Instead, I shall outline here some of the guiding presumptions which will be used throughout this introduction. Firstly, to call science fiction (SF) a genre causes problems because it does not recognize the hybrid nature of many SF works. It is more helpful to think of it as a mode or field where different genres and subgenres intersect. And then there is the issue of science. In the early decades of the 20th century, a number of writers attempted to tie this fiction to science and even to use it as a means of promoting scientific knowledge, a position which continues into what has become known as 'hard SF'. Applied science – technology – has been much more widely discussed in SF because every technological innovation affects the structure of our society and the nature of our behaviour. Technology has repeatedly been associated with the future by SF, but it does not follow that the fiction is therefore *about* the future. The crudest reading of an SF novel is to ask 'did Arthur C. Clarke get it wrong?' Science fiction is about the writer's present in the sense that any historical moment will include its own set of expectations and perceived tendencies. The futures represented in SF embody its speculative dimension. In that sense, as Joanna Russ has explained, it is a *'What If* Literature'. The writer and critic Samuel Delany has applied the term 'subjunctivity' to SF in a similar spirit to explain how these narratives position themselves between possibility and impossibility. It is helpful to think of an SF narrative as an embodied thought experiment whereby aspects of our familiar reality are transformed or suspended.

The heated debates about the nature of SF are usually conducted by its practitioners, and this can even be seen as one of the defining characteristics of the field. These exchanges often revolve around the status of SF, whether it consists of 'popular' or 'mainstream' fiction, despite the fact that such terms have increasingly lost their meaning in the sheer variety of contemporary published SF. Or the debates might centre on the history and scope of SF. The wave of feminist science fiction from the 1970s onwards also saw the retrospective construction of a tradition which rehabilitated writers like Charlotte Perkins Gilman. It has been a recurring claim among SF writers that they are more and more occupying the position previously occupied by realist fiction and that their narratives are the most engaged, socially relevant, and responsive to the modern technological environment. In a title that plays on Ariel's famous speech in *The Tempest*, Thomas M. Disch's *The Dreams Our Stuff Is Made Of* (1998) has argued that SF permeates every level of society, especially of the entertainment industry.

A *Very Short Introduction* cannot offer a history of SF, nor does it need to, since a number of excellent histories are currently in print. Instead, it will attempt to tie the selected examples to their different historical moments to demonstrate how science fiction has always been an evolving mode. There is extensive debate over when SF began. Some histories have extended their reach back as far as Lucian of Samosata's *A True Story* from the 2nd century

AD, which describes a voyage into space and a form of inter-planetary war. Other historians take their starting points in the Renaissance with works like Thomas More's *Utopia* (1516) and Francis Godwin's *The Man in the Moone* (1638), or in the Industrial Revolution with Mary Shelley's *Frankenstein* (1818). Two other starting points have been mooted: the late 19th century from around 1870, and the early 20th century when labels like 'science fiction' were first used. The latter position confuses descriptive labelling with the set of narrative practices which would necessitate such descriptions. Origination in antiquity raises different problems of cultural practice, and such examples could best be thought of as 'ur-SF'. Works from the Renaissance or early 19th century are clearly much closer to the methods we now identify with SF and could be described as 'proto-SF'. This is not to deny their self-evident importance to the evolution of SF, but it is common practice for literary historians and novelists themselves to seek precursors in their efforts to substantiate generic practice.

This volume will work on the premise that what we now know as science fiction began to emerge in the late 19th century with a great upsurge in utopias, future-war narratives, and representatives of other genres that can be grouped under the SF umbrella. Apart from the expansion in education which established a commercial base for a number of science fiction writers in Britain, the period from around 1870 through to the First World War was one of extraordinarily rapid technological change, with widespread use of electricity for the first time, the coming of aeroplanes, the development of the radio and cinema, and the proliferation of the popular press. It was also a period that saw the emergence of the USA as an imperial player on the world scene, with all the rivalry that carried with the older empires of Europe and Asia. During these years, we see the emergence of a body of writing with distinct preoccupations and characteristics that remains a recognizable, commercially viable, and sometimes very lucrative, feature of the culture industry. This body of work became known as science fiction.

The eagle-eyed reader will have spotted that all my examples so far, except for Lucian, have been British or American, and this volume will focus on Anglophone writing and will include such figures as Jules Verne and Stanisław Lem because they have been circulated around Anglophone cultures in translation. It has become a truism that the USA dominates the field of SF, although throughout this *Introduction* we shall see the recurrence of H. G. Wells as a formative, English figure in the development of science fiction. The majority of the selected examples will be taken from Britain and North America.

A final aspect of this *Introduction* should be noted. The label 'science fiction' actually covers work in a number of media. There is a substantial body of drama and poetry. The Science Fiction Poetry Association was founded in 1978. During the heyday in the 1920s and 1930s of the 'pulps', magazines printed on low-grade paper, science fiction comics made their appearance in the USA, developing rather later in Britain with publications like the *Eagle*. And then there are the SF games. War games were a special case, with their own history stretching back to military rehearsals in 19th-century Prussia, but since the 1980s there has been a boom in role-playing games drawing on newly available computer and virtual reality resources. We shall see in the final chapter that SF works since the 1970s, especially films, have produced a whole range of products under a common franchise. This introduction will focus primarily on print fiction but also on SF's twin medium – the cinema. No sooner had film been invented than experiments began with science fiction subjects, such as Georges Melies's *A Trip to the Moon* of 1902. The evolution of these two media has followed such parallel lines that since the Second World War many SF novels have received film adaptations.

The discussion that follows is broken down into six sections. The first examines voyages into space and other unexplored realms. The voyage embodies SF authors' imaginative outward reach, in the course of which they may encounter aliens, the subject of

Chapter 2. Here, the whole concept of the alien is examined, especially in the construction of alternative social identities. Chapter 3 moves on to the complex role of technology in SF, followed in Chapter 4 by a discussion of utopias and dystopias, which collectively make up one of the main traditions of SF. Chapter 5 addresses the relation of SF to time past as well as future, and Chapter 6 examines science fiction as a community of writers and critics constantly debating and modifying SF practice.

Chapter 1
Voyages into space

One of the first images we associate with science fiction is the spaceship; one of the first plot lines we expect is the journey into space, whose unlimited expanse licensed an outward reach of the novelists' imagination. Historically, there was an easy continuity between sea journeys such as that in Thomas More's *Utopia* or *Gulliver's Travels* and space flights. Both are represented as voyages, and both are innately serial because the action takes place between long periods of transition. Indeed, in early science fiction the use of anti-gravity devices was self-evidently a pretext for rapidly covering the enormous distances of space. Cyrano de Bergerac's twin narratives, *The States and Empires of the Moon* (1657) and *The States and Empires of the Sun* (unfinished at his death), both use a rocket journey from the Earth to set up their narratives, but it is no real concern of theirs to explain the technology of the rocket or the journeys, only the worlds at their destinations.

In these cases and in many subsequent works, the space voyage functions as a device for estranging us from the familiar world, enabling external (and usually ironic) perspectives to be set up on Earth. Thus Bergerac's traveller is forced in both cases to re-examine his presumptions about earthly values, and is considered by the Moon-dwellers to be little more than an ape. A later example shows the continuity between the two kinds of voyage. Joseph Atterley's *A Voyage to the Moon* (1827) describes how the son of an American merchant sets out on a voyage to Canton China, but is shipwrecked on the Burmese coast. Among his local companions, he befriends a Brahmin who reveals to him the secret of space travel and also the fact that the Moon has inhabitants. The two fly to the Moon in a copper cube, and the rest of the novel consists of the narrator's experiences of Moon culture under the guidance of the Brahmin, who points out the many differences from American society.

A last famous example will clarify the effect of transposition in such novels. David Lindsay's *A Voyage to Arcturus* (1920) once again gives only perfunctory attention to the voyage itself, the transit from Scotland to an inhabited star being effected by torpedo-shaped crystals. The action consists of a series of episodes in which the traveller Maskull experiences different kinds of perception on the new planet, such as that produced by growing a third eye. Here and in many other cases, the voyage into space offers convenient transit to other worlds, which offer sites for metaphysical and cultural speculation.

From an early stage in its development, science fiction showed a refreshing tendency to self-parody. Edgar Allen Poe is an important figure in the evolution of proto-SF and his hoax story 'The Unparalleled Adventure of One Hans Pfaall' (1835) draws on an already existing tradition of fabulous voyages beyond the Earth for comic effect. The story presents the 'edited' account by a Dutch scientist of how he flew to the Moon with the help of an air condenser, a kind of air-tight bag enclosing the apparatus. The pseudo-editorial frame to the story was a strategy used by writers to offset the amazing content of their narratives throughout the 19th century right up to H. G. Wells. Poe employs it to give a ludicrous credibility to his story which cleverly mimics scientific descriptions of the diminution of the Earth and increase in size of the Moon during the space voyage.

The supreme 19th-century novelist of travel remains Jules Verne, whose relation to science fiction continues to be a matter of debate. His *Voyages Extraordinaires* stories are not set in the future and cumulatively attempt to map out different areas of the globe. Travel is the key means towards this end. The duo of Verne novels most closely related to science fiction, *From the Earth to the Moon* and its sequel *Round the Moon* (both translated in 1873), pay tribute to Yankee inventiveness. A Gun Club is formed during the Civil War for the development of arms, and this impetus is tied in the novel to the imaginative appeal of getting to the Moon. Citing a medley of writers who blur the difference between fiction and non-fiction including Poe, Flammarion, and even the hoax essays of 1835 attributed to Herschel, the president of the Gun Club, Barbicane, announces the mission to the Moon by means of an enormous cannon. The projectile is named the Columbiad, which was already the name of a cannon in use by the US Army, but also carries epic associations articulated in Joel Barlow's 1807 poem of that name with the discoverer of America. The mission is an American enterprise supported by European capital raised on subscription. Once the launch has taken place from Florida, like the later Apollo missions, the novel hints at the possibility of life on the Moon, but the narrative gives priority to the spectacle of new views of the planets and lunar volcanoes. After the astronauts' successful return to Earth, plans are made to form the National Company of Interstellar Communication to set the commercial seal on subsequent voyages.

Hollow Earth

Imaginary explorations in early SF use three main settings: the Earth itself, near space, and the interior of the Earth. Although the concept had been used earlier for fantasy or satirical purposes, hollow Earth narratives developed in the late 19th century as a separate subgenre partly out of the theories of John Cleves Symmes Jr, who believed that the Earth had openings at the North and South Poles. This theory, popularly known as Symmes' Holes, was expressed in fictional form in Adam Seaborn's *Symzonia: A Voyage of Discovery* (1820), possibly written by Symmes himself. Towards the end of the century, there was a flurry of hollow Earth narratives, including Edward Bulwer-Lytton's *The Coming Race* (1871), in which a young American falls down a mine shaft and finds himself in a world which represents his imminent future. In this culture, women have become far more independent and a force resembling electricity called Vril (virile) is used by a master race.

Etidorhpa (i.e. Aphrodite), published in 1895, by John Uri Lloyd, a Cincinnati pharmacologist, is unique among hollow Earth narratives in not describing a separate civilization. Instead, it offers a surreal sequence of hallucinatory scenes. The story is elaborately framed as being told by a 'white-haired old man', who is kidnapped and transported to the centre of the Earth. One of his first sights is a 'fungus forest' of enormous multi-coloured mushrooms towering over him, and this sets the keynote of the novel, in which the traveller moves constantly between dreamlike states. The transitions are sudden and surreal, unrelated to any conceivable guided tour of this subterranean world. The shifts in dimension, and the attention to smells and sounds, have led some critics to suggest that *Etidorhpa* resembles a sequence of psychedelic visions.

Hollow Earth narratives tend to gloss over many of the physical difficulties of imagining within the Earth a world which would retain many of the characteristics of surface life. For instance, the interior location of Edgar Rice Burroughs' *Pellucidar* series (started in 1914) gives the reader his standard combination of 'primitive' races, tropical landscapes, and primeval creatures. Here, the terrain is used to justify the stream of exotic adventures confronting the protagonist and to embody the fantasy of travelling back into the evolutionary past, whereas other novels tie their action to the possibilities within the writer's present. William R. Bradshaw built his 1892 novel *The Goddess of*

Atvatabar on the publicity surrounding the Arctic exploration voyages of the time to describe the discovery of an inner world with sophisticated cultures. When civil war breaks out, an American-led expedition 'saves' the land for empire and opens up dazzling new vistas of commercial exploitation. The novel includes the exoticism common to most hollow Earth narratives, but makes unusually explicit the notion that this mysterious other world is ripe for conquest.

Science fiction and empire

John Rieder and other SF scholars have tied the emergence of SF towards the end of the 19th century with the heyday of empire. Rieder argues that from 1871 onwards, SF began to develop its own 'family of resemblances' which began to produce its identity as a genre. John Jacob Astor IV's *A Journey in Other Worlds* (1894) offers a clear example of the link between empire and space travel. Set in 2088, by which time the USA has achieved world hegemony, the narrative describes how the space traveller embarking on a voyage of exploration sees himself as continuing the national destiny of technological and territorial triumphs. As the flight progresses, his discoveries become progressively more fantastic: he finds mastodons on Jupiter, dragons and spirits on Saturn. At the end of the voyage, the spaceship flies home to a rapturous welcome. Astor's investment in empire was not confined to fiction. In 1898, he financed a battalion of volunteers to fight in Cuba during the Spanish-American War. Astor's nationalism reflects a general characteristic of turn-of-the-century exploration narratives, namely that they are never disinterested. Whether their ostensible motive is science or adventure, the ultimate desire for imperial appropriation is rarely far away.

Early in the 20th century, a subgenre of exploration emerged dealing with the discovery of lost worlds. Arthur Conan Doyle's *The Lost World* (1912) established the generic label and the pattern in describing how Professor Challenger discovers a plateau in the heart of the Amazon basin which contains living primeval creatures and primitive ape-men. Conan Doyle's narrative was followed in 1916 by Edgar Rice Burroughs' *The Land that Time Forgot*, repeating a similar discovery, this time in Antarctica. His hero encounters a creature resembling a man, but is he?

> I could not say, for it resembled an ape no more than it did a man. Its large toes protruded laterally as do the semiarboreal peoples of Borneo, the Philippines and other remote regions where low types still persist. The countenance might have been a cross between *Pithecanthropus*, the Java ape-man, and a daughter of the Piltdown race of prehistoric Sussex.

The traveller hesitates between past and present, although his uncertainty never shakes the implicit conviction of his evolutionary superiority. Lost-race fiction tends to present imperial exploration and discovery as adventure. The main popularizer of this subgenre was H. Rider Haggard with *King Solomon's Mines* (1885) and its sequels describing fabulous worlds hidden within the African interior. These narratives have been described as 'fantasies of appropriation', where the explorers act on territorial and sexual desire – a beautiful princess is a stock ingredient – and where invasion and conquest are systematically misrepresented as a return to their historical past or a recuperation of Nature's gifts. Lost-race tales could also be seen as stories of time travel in which explorers encounter earlier forms of humanity. In Conrad's *Heart of Darkness* (1902), Marlowe travels simultaneously into the heart of the African interior and back to the beginnings of evolutionary time. One of the most dramatic moments in his narrative occurs when he reluctantly recognizes a kinship with one of the natives. Clearly then, lost-world narratives anticipate a major theme in science fiction which will be dealt with in the following chapter – the alien encounter.

Space opera: star wars

By the logic of empire, the planets offer themselves for conquest, and so it is no coincidence that the first star wars novels in the language should be published during the heyday of empire. Indeed, the adventure paradigm central to space opera has been described as the 'myth-form of exploration and colonial conquest'. The anonymous *Man Abroad* (1887) describes an Earth already conquered by the USA. Settlers have flown in turn to the Moon, Venus, Mars, Jupiter, Saturn, and the asteroids. The novel sets a pattern for much subsequent SF in using the planets as hypothetical nations or colonies, displacing territorial disputes on to the Solar System. A trade dispute breaks out between the planets, but war never actually follows, unlike in Robert William Cole's *The Struggle for Empire* (1900). This novel starts in the year 2236 and evokes a cosmic Pax Britannica, that is, a world dominated by the Anglo-Saxons, who have invented a means of space travel in 'interstellar ships'. War breaks out between Earth and Sirius, whose inhabitants resemble humans in every respect, but who possess a more advanced military technology. The massive Sirian fleet of airships roll back empire to its centre and London is bombarded. It seems that the fate of London and the whole empire is sealed, until a British scientist invents a device for projecting force-waves which suddenly and decisively reverses the course of the war. The Anglo-Saxons re-conquer space and bomb the Sirian capital city, bringing speedy capitulation.

These early projections of empire on to space set the pattern for the 'space opera' stories which began to appear in the pulps between the wars. The phrase 'space opera' was coined in 1941 to label hack science fiction and it kept its negative meaning until the 1980s, when it was redefined to mean SF adventure narratives. In that period, space opera went through a revival, with writers like Iain M. Banks, David Brin, and Dan Simmons modifying the subgenre in more sophisticated narrative forms. Between the world wars, two space opera narratives have a special significance. The first was a pair of linked stories by Philip Francis Nowlan from 1928–9 in which he introduced the character of Anthony Rogers, soon renamed Buck for the comic strip which followed.

The composite volume *Armageddon 2419 AD* describes how our hero falls asleep at a point when the USA is the most powerful

1. Cover for *Buck Rogers in the 25th Century AD* (1933)

nation in the world and wakes in the 25th century to find his country in ruins, ruled by the ruthless Han. Nowlan's tale is essentially a Yellow Peril story with futuristic weapons added. What follows is a struggle to restore freedom to the USA and the rest of the world, and to defeat once and for all 'that monstrosity among the races of men', the Chinese. We shall see in a moment why the Buck Rogers franchise should have been revived and developed in the 1970s. The second formative narrative dates from the same period, E. E. 'Doc' Smith's *The Skylark in Space* (1928). This work helped to establish the stereotypical hero of space opera. Richard Seaton is a scientist, athlete, and a 'born fighter', in short a clean-cut man of action. The novel opens with his discovery of a force making space travel possible, which leads to the construction of a spaceship, the *Skylark* of the title. It is a mark of the modernity of treatment that the craft needs commercial construction rather than individual enthusiasm, as was the case in earlier accounts of space flight. Every hero needs a villain, and this role is played by an unscrupulous representative of the World Steel Corporation who builds a duplicate ship and flies into space carrying with him the hapless Dorothy, Seaton's girlfriend. The first half of the novel describes Seaton's pursuit of this craft and rescue of Dorothy. From then on, the *Skylark* flies to different planets, some inhabited by races themselves possessing sophisticated airships. After a series of adventures following the Burroughs formula of captivity and escape, our hero returns safely to Earth with his companions.

Taken together, these two works helped establish the characteristics of space opera: the idealized male hero; futuristic weaponry like ray-guns; an episodic action full of the exotic and unexpected; and a struggle between starkly opposed forces for good and evil. These were drawn on by George Lucas for his 1977 film *Star Wars*, which combined Buck Rogers with battle scenes from Kurosawa, and which drew on Joseph Campbell's study *The Hero with a Thousand Faces* for its plot line. The *Star Wars* franchise has been one of the biggest commercial successes ever, and in addition to the film sequels and prequels has included other films, some animated; many novels in subseries within the broader narrative, as well as guides to the individual films; comic books; and a whole range of computer and video games. The 1960s television series *Star Trek* was also partly suggested by the Buck Rogers stories, but was constructed as a continuous, open-ended voyage through space by the *US Starship Enterprise*, whose mission was, in the words of one of the series catch-phrases, 'to boldly go where no man has gone before'. SF writers like Harlan Ellison and Theodore Sturgeon were brought in to write episodes, which were usually built around an encounter; the first in the series concerned a meeting in space with an alien craft manned by a childlike being. Like the *Star Wars* series, *Star Trek* too produced several subsequent television series and a large number of novels and novelizations.

Harry Harrison parodies the militarism and masculinism in space opera in *Bill, the Galactic Hero* (1965), a futuristic retelling of Jaroslav Hasek's *The Good Soldier Schweik*. Here, Bill gets inducted into the star troopers purely by chance, though he protests that he is 'not the military type', and embarks on a picaresque series of farcical mishaps, where he demonstrates none of the traditional heroic qualities associated with that fiction. In a similar spirit, the Polish author Stanisław Lem created his cosmonaut Ijon Tichy, who describes his experiences of time loops, galactic administrative gatherings, and adventures on other planets in a dead-pan understated prose which implicitly satirizes the whole desire for heroic action in space opera.

Spaceships

From Georges Melies's 1902 film *A Trip to the Moon* onwards, the spaceship became one of the key icons of SF, with its sleek rocket design, promising freedom and escape. Fritz Lang's *Woman in the Moon* (1928) described a voyage which finally left two lovers stranded on the Moon.

2. Poster for Fritz Lang's *Frau im Mond* (1929)

In the last scene, they embrace in a romantic climax which will signal their imminent death. This film first used the countdown to launch, as noted in Thomas Pynchon's novel about the V-2 rockets *Gravity's Rainbow* (1973), and drew on the services of the rocket engineer Hermann Oberst for technical advice. In Edwin Balmer and Philip Wylie's 1933 novel *When Worlds Collide*, it functions as a saving vessel. Two rogue planets are discovered to be heading towards Earth, and as one approaches the signs of disaster multiply: massive tidal waves, extraordinary winds, and sudden fires. A spaceship is constructed to take a saving remnant out of danger. Once launched, the passengers witness the destruction of Earth, but discover that the second planet is actually inhabitable. Not only that; the new Earth shows traces of habitation and the novel ends on an upbeat note of fresh beginnings, whose optimism blanks out the countless practical questions of how they will survive.

Throughout the first half of the 20th century, the space voyage became one of the staple ingredients of science fiction. One of the most famous novels to use this pattern was A. E. Van Vogt's *The Voyage of Space Beagle* (1950, a 'fix-up' from previous short stories), whose title echoes Charles Darwin's naturalist journal of his travels round the world, *The Voyage of Beagle* (1839). The purpose of Van Vogt's voyage is scientific exploration for the Nexial Foundation, and he applies a Darwinian presumption that contact with other species will produce conflict. The *Space Beagle* undergoes four encounters, of decreasing materiality: first with a cat-like creature, then with telepathic birds, and a creature living in space wanting to implant eggs in a human host, finally with a consciousness at large in space. A number of Van Vogt's episodes feature in narratives of alien encounter. His novel was also one of the first to describe a spaceship crew working together.

An important revision of the traditional image of the spaceship was made in Anne McCaffrey's Helva stories, beginning in 1961 with *The Ship Who Sang*. This series is set in a future when severely disabled children are given the chance to become starships by becoming enclosed in a metal shell connected directly to their brain. This is an enabling procedure involving 'schooling' (not programming) and complex neural and sensory connections being constructed through the titanium shell. In this respect, the 'shell-people' represent an early form of cyborg, and McCaffrey's narrative replaces central technological control with the individual investigations and self-modifications by Helva herself in devising a means of singing. Flight for her is depicted as a coming-of-age adventure rather than an overtly directed scientific voyage. Helva's shell functions as an extension of her consciousness, so that she simultaneously demonstrates technical skill in her flights through space – up to the 1960s the monopoly of male pilots – and at the same time develops her emotional capacity, for example to learn how to mourn. Similarly, Naomi Mitchison's *Memoirs of a Spacewoman* (1962) replaces rapid action with a reflective sequence on the relation of the narrator to other species.

2001: A Space Odyssey

Arthur C. Clarke has consistently championed space exploration, promoting it as a defining activity of the second half of the 19th century. As early as 1946, he was prophesying a new age of exploration, and in 1962 speculated on the possible revival, if not of epic, then at least of something approaching it: 'surely the discoveries and adventures, the triumphs and inevitable tragedies that must accompany man's drive toward the stars will one day inspire a new heroic literature'. Clarke consistently stressed science fiction's unique capacity to evoke wonder and to inspire readers with large visions. Thus when spaceships appear over the world's cities in *Childhood's End* (1953), the story sounds like the script of a B-movie from that decade – until contact begins with the aliens. Clarke minimizes the newcomers' appearance except to stress their size, which is the physical correlative of their mental superiority. The Overlords begin to produce children on Earth who have new telepathic abilities and are clearly being used by

Clarke as a catalyst to help humanity evolve into a more rational phase. In that sense, the novel cleared the ground for Clarke's most famous voyage narrative, *2001: A Space Odyssey* (1968).

Clarke wrote the novel as Stanley Kubrick's film was evolving, unlike many later novelizations of SF movies. The space flight which makes up the majority of novel and film grows out of a preliminary Wellsian narrative of human technological progress. The primitive protagonist at this point is named Moon-Watcher to set up space travel as an instinctive purpose from the very beginning. The brief summary of Darwinian evolution (development of tools and weapons for self-defence in the struggle for existence) shifts into the year 1999, a transition marked imagistically in the film as a bone thrown into the air mutates into a space station. By this year, a ferry service to the Moon has become commonplace, but the drama begins with the excavation of a mysterious black slab which transmits a signal towards Saturn. Jump forward again to 2001, and the main voyage begins with the mission of *Discovery One* to Saturn, manned by two astronauts, Bowman and Poole.

Apart from the obvious epic analogy in the title, Clarke punctuates the novel with references to famous voyages of the past, as if to

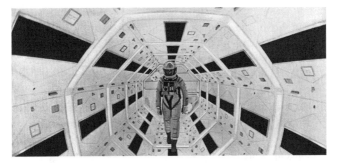

3. Still from Stanley Kubrick's *2001: A Space Odyssey* (1968)

suggest that the present one is a culmination of human enterprise. The final title evoked a grander theme than the original one, *Beyond the Stars*. However, the voyage runs into difficulties. A unit apparently malfunctions and HAL, the onboard computer, opens the airlocks, causing the death of Poole. It is then revealed that the real purpose of the mission is to explore Japetus, one of Saturn's moons; in the film, the aim was to reach Jupiter.

The surreal culmination to the voyage comes when *Discovery One* reaches Japetus and Bowman enters a monolith identical to that on the Moon. As he approaches his target, he sees a kind of parking lot of derelict spacecraft, then a phantasmagoria of brilliant light spots, until he suddenly finds himself in a Washington hotel suite. By this time, the action has become more hallucinatory, as if based on the ground of his mind. Objects come in and out of focus, Bowman's consciousness passes through a threshold 'stargate', and the narrative finishes with an image of rebirth full of spiritual associations. Kubrick has stated that 'the concept of God is at the heart of *2001*', a sentiment confirmed by Clarke. For Kubrick, the spiritual symbolism of the film was left deliberately vague to allow viewers to project their different interpretations on to it, and the ending itself has at least three different phases: arrival at destination, regression to the past, and the imminent emergence of a new birth. Clarke was to return to the ambiguous spiritual symbolism of spacecraft in *Rendezvous with Rama* (1973), in which a huge cylindrical spaceship named *Rama* approaches the Earth. Exploratory missions are sent to examine it, but from its sheer size, it has to be mapped as if it were a miniature planet. Despite its evident technological sophistication and the presence within it of cybernetic 'biots', at the end of the novel *Rama* leaves the Solar System without anyone on Earth being clear about its purpose. Clarke underlines this ambiguity through references to Christianity, Hinduism, and Greek mythology. The vessel might be a spiritual visitation; then again, it might not.

The US space programme

The 1969 Apollo 11 landing on the Moon radically altered the tradition of space exploration in science fiction by transforming our sense of possibility. This event, together with the unmanned probes to Mars and Venus, made it no longer possible to ignore science in narratives of space exploration. The National Aeronautics and Space Administration (NASA) now routinely uses SF material in its educational facility on space technology, and a number of its staff are SF authors in their own right. In 2004, NASA held its first debate about terraforming Mars with SF authors including Arthur C. Clarke and Kim Stanly Robinson. Robert Zubin, founder of the Mars Society, has supplemented his campaigning for Mars exploration with a 2001 novel *First Landing*, about the discovery of biological life on that planet. The novelists dealing with the subject of Mars, often themselves trained scientists, make strenuous efforts to harmonize their narratives with known scientific advances. One option used by Ben Bova is to provide a separate 'Data Bank' of information relevant to the story in his novels. The astrophysicist Gregory Benford prefers instead to incorporate the science into the narrative proper. *The Martian Race* (1999) puns on the possibility of life on Mars – central to this fiction – and the new arrangements for financing a voyage following the disastrous explosion on launch of a craft which leads to the withdrawal of congressional support. A consortium offers $30 billion to whoever can first achieve a successful Mars mission. Part of the novel describes the jockeying for publicity and funding on Earth; part describes the conduct of scientific investigation of the Martian landscape and the discovery of organisms by Julia Barth, the biologist protagonist. But there is a third element which prevents the novel from being simply another example of 'hard' SF. During the narrative, Benford's characters reference the antecedents of the novel in earlier treatments of Mars, notably *The Creeping Unknown* (the US title of *The Quatermass Experiment*, 1955), in which an astronaut becomes infected by an organism in space, and *Mars Needs Women* (1968), a joking allusion to Benford's own protagonist. Once the organisms start growing, the action darkens and there is even a suggestion of a humanoid growth taking shape which might threaten the crew. In this way, Benford manages to straddle both the older imagined scenarios of extraterrestrial life and the new scientific discoveries on that planet.

Robinson, Bova, and Benford represent a positive view of the space programme which was in fact the subject of controversy in its early stages. As early as 1956, James Blish had scathingly criticized a government system that both centralizes control and compartmentalizes research workers on such a programme and cuts them off from each other for reasons of national 'security'. A later negative depiction of space exploration is Barry Malzberg's *Beyond Apollo* (1972), the narrated plans for a novel by the sole survivor of a mission to Venus, whose sanity is constantly in doubt.

Inner space

In the SF journal *New Worlds* for 1962, J. G. Ballard made his famous protest against the hegemony of the 'rocket and planet story' in science fiction. Despite, or perhaps because of, the then current space race between the USA and Soviet Union, he argued that SF was in need of a new direction and declared: 'The biggest developments of the immediate future will take place, not on the Moon or Mars, but on Earth, and it is *inner* space, not outer, that needs to be explored.' In place of its traditional emphasis on science, he continued, he would prefer a move towards abstraction: 'instead of treating time like a sort of glorified scenic railway, I'd like to see it used for what it is, one of the perspectives of the personality, and the elaboration of concepts such as the time zone, deep time and archaeopsychic time'. Ballard's rejection of traditional space stories was shared by a number of his contemporaries, though their practice took different directions. Michael Moorcock made extensive use of willed time travel, and Douglas Adams began his Hitchhiker series (originally a science fiction radio comedy) with *The Hitchhiker's Guide to the Galaxy* (1979), reducing space to an area which can be traversed as casually as hitching a lift.

In fact, well before Ballard's declaration, there had been some signs of change. One of the first novels to apply the discovery of atomic structure to fiction was Ray Cummings's *The Girl in the Golden Atom* (1922), published soon after he stopped working as an assistant to Edison. Here, the dimension of space is given a new limit as a scientist reveals to his bemused friends the discovery of a whole world inside a single atom. There is an element of erotic fantasy in this, since, by massively magnifying his mother's wedding ring, he glimpses a beautiful young girl sitting in a cave. Like the bottles from which Alice drinks in Wonderland, the scientist devises a chemical capable of either reducing or magnifying a creature's size. In this narrative, change in size replaces travel, but produces unexpected results in that, as the chemist shrinks, the objects of the real world become huge and threatening. He enters a surreal world of shifting planes and sudden precipices, and finds himself in constant danger from the magnified forms of the objects and beings he has not left behind. Having established these stark differences of dimension, Cummings then moves the narrative on into yet another lost-world story, where the two races within the atom are at loggerheads with each other.

Only four years after Ballard's call for change, Richard Fleischer relocated the voyage paradigm by situating it within a human body. *Fantastic Voyage* (1966) uses the Cold War to motivate its action. When a Soviet scientist who has been experimenting with techniques of miniaturization escapes to the West, an attempted assassination leaves him with a blood clot in the brain. To save his life, a small crew aboard the submarine *Proteus* are reduced to the size of what would now be called a nanobot and sail through the scientist's blood vessels, eventually finding the clot. The action is complicated by a member of the crew being a Communist agent but, in a race against time, the clot is removed and the crew escape from the body through the eyes. Despite the absurdity of the subject, rather less now than when it was released because of subsequent medical miniaturization techniques, the film evoked new surreal 'bodyscapes', internal images of human organs vastly magnified. This film was further developed by the 1987 comedy *Innerspace*, in which an experiment to miniaturize a human subject for an experimental injection into a rabbit goes wrong and the action turns into a struggle between rival agencies for the technology.

Within the context of 1960s drug experimentation, Ballard's statements about inner space harmonized with the convention of descriptions of drug experiences being located 'inside'. Brian Aldiss's *Barefoot in the Head* (1969) remains a powerful application of this concept in its description of a post-war world after bombs have been dropped releasing hallucinogenic substances; the stories in this volume were originally published as the 'Acid Head War' series. The protagonist Colin Charteris, whose name echoes the creator of the fictional Saint, is in fact a Serb travelling through Western Europe into Britain. Once there, the effect of the hallucinogens in the atmosphere makes reality start warping unpredictably so that space and time become destabilized. Aldiss even applies this effect to the text itself, which moves in and out of narrative, and constantly relates Charteris's experiences to a general breakdown in European society.

In Judith Merril's 1968 anthology *England Swings SF*, she combines the metaphors of science fiction and drug-taking by presenting her contributors as going on a 'trip' and sailing a 'scout ship' to unknown destinations. This process could be the result of conscious experimentation, as happens in the early fiction of William Burroughs, who prided himself on his expert knowledge of mind-altering drugs. One of his major concerns was with control, and he repeatedly drew on science fiction to express his conviction that a human being was a 'soft machine', an organism connected to some agency of control which he designates the 'reality studio'. In *The Soft Machine* (1961, 1966), he evokes an attack on this studio as an attempt to wrest back control of inner space. His trope of the 'reality film' implies the already-constructed nature of reality, which we will find recurring in the fiction of Philip K. Dick and others.

In his original call for explorations of inner space, Ballard primarily suggests a turn away from tales of space journeys and not necessarily a move towards psychological exploration. Since his 1962 statement, the very notion of inner space has gone through a series of transformations, including visual mapping, internal microscopic imagery, and of course cyberspace, a term defined in 1982 by the SF novelist William Gibson and famously explained in *Neuromancer* (1984) as a:

> consensual hallucination experienced daily by billions of legitimate operators, in every nation, by children being taught mathematical concepts . . . A graphic representation of data abstracted from banks of every computer in the human system. Unthinkable complexity. Lines of light ranged in the nonspace of the mind, clusters and constellations of data. Like city lights, receding.

Cyberspace can only be explained paradoxically as simultaneously space and non-space, now closely identified with the Internet and World Wide Web, both expressions carrying embedded metaphors of concretized systems of information transfer. The verb 'to surf' the Web adds an even more quasi-physical dimension to information searching.

However, it is the particular phrase 'virtual reality' (VR) that connects most directly with fictional representations of space. Dating again primarily from the 1980s, VR was promoted as an electronic recreational drug. In 1990, the *Wall Street Journal* described it as 'electronic LSD', an analogy demonstrated in the character Visual Mark in Pad Cadigan's 1991 novel *Synners*. Mark is a VR junkie dreaming of an escape from limits or boundaries so that 'he could fly through the universe if he wanted to'. Cadigan gives brilliantly vivid description of the totally immersive experience of donning a 'video head', an electronic VR helmet and also an obvious pun on addiction. The character Gina dons one of these and promptly begins to experience odd shifts of sensation and time, losing control over what happens and when. The rapid transformation of scenes and their shifts in duration recall the dreamscapes of De Quincey's *Confessions of an English Opium-Eater* (1821). Indeed, when Gina emerges from her VR 'trip', it is described as if she wakes. In Neal Stephenson's *Snow Crash* (1992), by contrast, place is shared as the Street, the avenue of information transactions in what he calls the 'Multiverse', a term originally coined by William James to suggest the variety of Nature, here suggesting the pluralization and malleability of reality itself.

Chapter 2
Alien encounters

Science fiction constantly interrogates the limits of identity and the nature of difference. The latter is frequently described through a quasi-allegorical displacement of the alien on to other countries and planets, following a strategy of encounter whereby readers are encouraged to re-examine their self-conceptions as a result of confrontation with the Other, with beings whose culture is rarely explored in its own right, but rather to highlight the markers of difference.

The concept of the alien in science fiction could be understood in three overlapping senses. It could refer to startlingly different beings, sometimes from other planets; it could refer to social estrangement like the class polarities between the underground workers and the decadent pleasure-seekers of H. G. Wells's *The Time Machine* (1895) or between the managerial elite and the zombified workers in *Metropolis*; or again, it could refer to a quality of the narrative itself, which up to the beginning of the 20th century was often introduced to the reader through a quasi-editorial frame. It is possible to find all these qualities in one volume. The American Pierton W. Dooner's *Last Days of the Republic* (1880), for instance, transforms the use of Chinese immigrant labour into a conspiracy. Inverting the providential confidence of Manifest Destiny, Dooner externalizes the impulse to dominate on to the Chinese, who gradually take over the USA, with the final result that its very name disappears from the map.

The very term 'alien' suggests otherness and difference. The aliens in science fiction are by definition always imagined through reference to familiar human groups, animal species, or machines. Two of the earliest occurrences of the term 'alien' are in Edgar Rice Burroughs's *A Princess of Mars* (1912), in which his hero Captain John Carter of the Confederate army escapes attack by Apaches in Arizona when he is mysteriously transported to Mars. On the Red Planet, he is observing the customs of the green race of humanoids. He gazes at their 'alien incubator', which is a kind of nest where the infant Martians are reared. Here, the adjective marks a difference from human practice in that there are no parents in the green race. The second occurrence is rather different. Carter has become accepted by one of the Martian races, although a leader declares his surprise to the visitor, stating 'You are an alien' but at the same time a chieftain. The very fact that the Martian can speak and even apply the term to Carter reverses its meaning back to the human original. In other words, alien-ness can be a shifting relation dependent upon context and perspective. During the period between the wars, the term 'alien' became attached more and more to extraterrestrial beings, but we should remember that it had earlier roots in 19th-century race theory and politics. Hostility to aliens was institutionalized in the USA by the Chinese Exclusion Act (1882) and Anarchist Exclusion Act (1901).

In this same period, quasi-humans on Mars – the favourite possibility at the turn of the 19th century – tended to be described in terms consistent with the racial hierarchy of the period. In Percy Greg's *Across the Zodiac* (1880), short humans are discovered on Mars who have an Aryan appearance like Swedes or Germans. And Gustavus W. Pope, in his *Journey to Mars* (1894), conveniently colour-codes his own Martians into red, yellow, and blue races. And to return to Burroughs, his Barsoom series provides perhaps the most famous early description of life on Mars. In *A Princess of Mars*, John Carter's first sight is of grotesque creatures hatching that have large heads and atrophied limbs. While he is gazing at these animals, a band of warriors ride up and carry him away with them. Already, the sliding scale of alienness is moving towards the human because, although the green men have two extra limbs, their culture distantly resembles that of the Native Americans, according to perceptions of the time. Burroughs planned his first Mars novel to depict a 'scientific race of dominant Martians', who were to resemble humans. He uses Mars as a fantasy site on which he can assemble creatures nearer or farther from humanity. The first creatures Carter sees form part of the exotic backdrop of the planet. The conflicts between the green and the red people resemble earthly conflicts between 'advanced' and 'primitive' peoples, to use the terms of his period.

In *The Gods of Mars* (1918), Burroughs added another race to his planet, the 'plant people', who are one-eyed, hairless, with displaced mouths in the palms of their hands. Miniature versions of this creature dangle from its armpits. As with the first volume, the most grotesque image of Mars comes first. The subsequent creatures all seem relatively odd rather than monstrous in comparison. The great white apes suggest an earlier evolutionary phase. The 'red men', actually possessing a copper-coloured complexion, suggest the conventional 19th-century colour-coding of the Native Americans. Finally, the 'black pirates' were designed to be the 'primeval' but 'pure' race of Mars, the aristocracy among the other races. In appearance, they present a collective embodiment of the noble savage, differing from Carter's people only in colour. Odd as it might seem for a Southerner, Carter has to admit that their colour adds to their beauty. The textual cues Burroughs gives us in his novels suggest that we read among earthly resemblances and differences, responding to his aliens, whose actions establish a rhythm of captivity and escape that became the hallmark of Burroughs's narratives.

We have so far been considering humanoid figures, but the alien could also be of a different species altogether, as happens in H. G. Wells's *The First Men in the Moon* (1901). The first Selenite that Wells's travellers see is an ant-person, a 'complicated insect' carrying a body case with 'goggles' and 'spikes' on his head. They cannot agree whether they are seeing a kind of man or not because 'he' is a hybrid creature, physically resembling a large ant, but possessing intelligence and technology, as they realize when taken captive. The two escape but only one manages to make his way back to Earth. Wells strikes a careful balance between not over-emphasizing the Selenites' appearance and evoking their social organization. This care tends to lapse in the SF stories in the pulp magazines, where bug-eyed monsters became common. This phrase has passed into cliché, usually suggesting threatening creatures of other or indeterminate species characterized by aggression, or lust for the hapless female characters unfortunate enough to encounter them. The art work of the prolific SF illustrator Frank R. Paul on the covers of these magazines played its part. We can see a clear example in Figure 4, where dwarfed humans flee before a monstrous creature with multiple limbs and a head indistinct from its torso.

In Stanley Weinbaum's *A Martian Odyssey* (1934), a new possibility for the alien emerges, where 'he' is simultaneously different and similar. On a first expedition to Mars, travellers meet anthropoids and a 'freak ostrich'. This creature is introduced by stressing its otherness, then its appearance is progressively reduced in oddity so that it might conceivably belong in the same species as the humans. Finally, it is not really a bird, just a creature with a small round body and long neck. More importantly, it demonstrates clear signs of intelligence: it can understand maths diagrams and gradually learns English. It is named as Tweel and becomes a companion, sharing the sights of Mars together with the humans. The more Tweel becomes humanized, the less his appearance is remarked upon.

4. Cover for *Amazing Stories* (May 1928)

Alien invasions

In the decades following the Second World War, the crude
monsters of the pulps became transformed into a whole range of
creatures whose actions were presented as invasive and
threatening. Alien invasion narratives tend to raise one stark issue:

conquer or be conquered. But their subtleties often lay in the strategies used to delay their revelation of the aliens, for they have to be seen and identified before they can be resisted. In evoking such diverse threats to humans, these narratives overlap constantly with the Gothic.

Among British examples, the television series *The Quatermass Experiment* (1955) dramatized contact with aliens as an infection. A rocket crashes on Wimbledon Common bearing a sole astronaut who is carrying an absorptive virus. Carroon, the astronaut, is traumatized and has great difficulty remembering what happened, which remains a mystery. A sequence of images begins with 'some sort of jelly' found in the rocket, through a grey inhuman hand as Carroon begins to mutate, culminating in a whole creature which materializes in Westminster Abbey, where it is finally destroyed. The second Quatermass series and the film *Quatermass 2* (1957) describe more of an invasion than the first. Mysterious objects are picked up on radar falling to Earth. When some of the objects are examined, they prove to be hollow vessels, presumably carriers of some sort. Investigating the area where they fell, Quatermass, the central scientist, comes across a mysterious industrial plant, apparently built by the government and barred to visitors as top secret. As author Nigel Kneale later recalled, he was playing here to fears in the mid-1950s of official bureaucracy and secret installations. As in the first series, suspense is built up by reports of a strange illness affecting people living near the plant, whose guards are called 'zombies' by the locals because of their masked, insect-like appearance. It is finally revealed that the plant is manufacturing synthetic food for the organisms that have dropped from the sky. Quatermass pursues them back to their home asteroid and destroys them. The US title for the film, significantly, was *Enemy from Space*.

The most powerful British narratives of alien invasion in the 1950s came from John Wyndham, who followed a strategy of embedding his science fiction subjects in the circumstantial detail of daily life. *The Day of the Triffids* (1951) presents two simultaneous threats to humanity: one extraterrestrial, the other organic. The triffids originate from a biological experiment conducted in the Soviet Union, their spores being dropped on Britain in an apparent air accident. It is no coincidence that contemporary fears had been expressed in the news of satellites dropping biological weapons on Britain. The second 'attack' comes from green shooting stars which blind all those who have been watching them. The nation has thus been collectively disabled and displaced from its position of species superiority, and as a result laid open to the assault of the triffids which gathers head in the second part of the novel.

5. **Sketch illustrating John Wyndham's *The Day of the Triffids* (1951)**

Brian Aldiss has accused Wyndham of creating 'cosy catastrophes', but this charge does no justice to Wyndham's understated method, no doubt partly aimed at avoiding the melodramatics of space opera narratives. The narrator interprets both assaults retrospectively as revealing the complacency of the British, hence the gloom of his account, which is peppered with numerous references to death and endings. *The Kraken Wakes* (1953) repeats the invasion motif, this time by strange organisms that have dropped in the oceans from the sky. In a bid to kill some of them off, the British detonate a nuclear device which has the reverse effect of bringing them to life. In other words, the invasion of sea creatures results directly from the failure of the British nuclear device.

The 'mentality' of the triffids or the sea creatures is never known. In *The Midwich Cuckoos* (1957), however, we have a quasi-human invasion of a village representative of middle England. Reports of an unidentified flying object over the village of the title are followed by a mysterious blank-out of the village, during which time all women of child-bearing age are impregnated. The resulting children all bear an uncanny resemblance to each other, having identical composite features, which leads the narrator to describe them as abstractly 'foreign', without any similarity to another race. An unusual moment of self-reflexive commentary occurs in this novel when a character spells out the American paradigm of invasion fiction in order to suggest differences from British accounts, stressing the speed of the action and the last-minute reprieve ending.

The pattern of US alien invasion movies of the 1950s was rather more complex than Wyndham's character suggests, however. Typically, an object, mistakenly thought to be a meteor, crashes near a small town. The beings inside it use the site of the crash (an old mine, sandpit, or other location) as a base from which to take over their human subjects. This might be through substitution (*I Married a Monster from Outer Space*, 1958); infection (*The*

Brain Eaters, also 1958); or take-over. In *Invaders from Mars* (1953), the victims receive a small implant in their neck which is used by their 'director' to sabotage nearby military installations. In the last, it is only a little boy who senses what is taking place, and the film makes extensive use of upward shots from his point of view. The threat is presented most crudely in *The Blob* (1958), in which a growing amoeba-like organism simply absorbs its human subjects; or in an unexpected way, as happens in *It Came from Outer Space* (1953, based on a script by Ray Bradbury). Here, the film follows the pattern of invasion, with the locals of an Arizona town being absorbed by a kind of large mobile bubble, and then it is revealed that the aliens are after all benign, only there to repair their spaceship. In most cases, the aliens land near a small town, whose fate by implication reflects that of the nation at large.

In Robert Heinlein's *The Puppet Masters* (1951), the national scale to the action is explicit from the very beginning. In the year 2007, a mysterious spacecraft lands near Grinnell, Iowa. So far it sounds like a conventional UFO story, but that pays no attention to the role of the narrator. Sam is a member of a secret government agency working under someone simply referred to as the 'Old Man', who is so important that he has a direct line to the President. That fact in itself forewarns us that no ordinary action is taking place. As happens in invasion movies, local communications are broken, and then reports start leaking out of altered behaviour. In addition, Sam fills in the historical context of UFO sightings dating from the 1940s – the first publicized viewings of a UFO took place near Washington in 1947 – and a nuclear war which has already taken place between the USA and Russia. The twinned themes of war and national threat inflate the action of the novel as soon as it gets under way. It emerges that the alien agency is a multiplying number of slug-like creatures who attach themselves to the backs of their victims and from that point on control them. Heinlein combines ancient fears of possession, revulsion, and political threat in these creatures, who even take over Sam for a brief period. He is reduced to a mechanism, the passive instrument of an anonymous director guiding him how to make contacts and 'secure' a building. The military term appropriately reflects what is in effect a subversion of the USA from within. Sam mentions posthypnotic suggestion as an analogue of what is happening to him, and the novel was published just when the first reports of brainwashing were coming back from the Korean War. If the slugs begin to resemble popular fears of Communist infiltration, Heinlein draws explicit parallels with the Soviet Union as the action expands across the nation and awkwardly designates the slugs 'titans' despite their size. Military combat proves useless against them, and so a virus is spread through infected slugs which ultimately saves the nation.

This pattern was not followed at all in the most famous alien invasion movie of the decade, *Invasion of the Body Snatchers* (1956), based on Jack Finney's 1955 novel *The Body Snatchers*. Despite being a low-budget production, the film powerfully dramatized the changes taking place in a small California town after mysterious pods start producing human duplicates which replace their originals. As is the case with similar films of the period, the means of the invasion (spores drifting though space) is far less important than its result, which is the gradual estrangement of the point-of-view character, Miles Bennell, the town doctor, from people he has known for years. The pods function as an agency of disruption, producing humanoid 'blanks' who then take on the detailed form of town members. Once the change has taken place, it is very difficult to recognize that they are not the characters they simulate. In this respect, *The Invasion* makes a striking positive contrast with other invasion narratives of the period in which the quality of the alien is usually observable in a zombification of the victims. In *The Invasion*, the transformation of more and more familiar figures is presented as a process inducing the paranoid fear in Miles that he can no longer recognize anyone. Jack Finney's original novel paces the revelation of this process as one of gradually mounting drama,

6. Poster for Don Siegel's *Invasion of the Body Snatchers* (1956)

whereas in the film Don Siegel added a frame which introduces urgency right from the very beginning when Miles is admitted to the emergency ward of the local hospital. It is the difference between the gradual discovery of crisis in the novel, and its immediate introduction and substantiation in the film.

The producer Walter Wanger originally planned to open the film with a calculated echo of the 1938 radio broadcast of *The War of the Worlds*. Orson Welles was to speak in his own voice as if reporting on events in the town. He was to have delivered lines like 'this is no ordinary world we are living in', as if cuing in the audience's acceptance of paranormal events. In the event, this plan was dropped, perhaps because it introduced the science fiction dimension of the action too explicitly. Instead, the film shows the relentless isolation of Miles and his girlfriend Becky as the police and local telephone exchange are taken over, culminating in their pursuit by the rest of the townsfolk towards the end of the film. The added frame reverses the position of Miles from doctor to patient, suggesting right up to the last scene that maybe the action was a hallucination. When a traffic accident verifies his story, the film closes with the hospital authorities calling the FBI. Each of the film's subsequent remakes alters the location of the action: the 1978 version is set in San Francisco, starting with urban alienation even before the pods get into action; the 1993 *Body Snatchers* uses an Alabama army base; and *The Invasion* (2007) shows the alien life form entering the Earth on a space shuttle and starting an epidemic of DNA transformations. Opinions continue to divide over what the original pods represent. Some see the action as an encoded expression of fear of Communism, repeatedly demonized in the period as producing mindless obedience to authority. Others have seen the narrative as a parable of social conformity in general.

A recurring analogy in alien invasions is with disease, as if the new life form was somehow corrupting or infecting its human host. William Burroughs, whose fiction draws on many SF tropes, has constructed his own grand narrative, a new mythology for the space age, that language itself carries a virus which 'would infect the entire population and turn them into our replicas', as a speaker for this non-human agency puts it. In this scenario, every individual is a potential carrier of this virus from outer space and the very medium for communicating infection – words – are themselves carriers. This must be the ultimate in paranoia, where the very medium for examining and confronting the virus is itself already infected.

Unlike Burroughs's alien, which is imperceptible and shapeless, Ridley Scott's 1979 film *Alien* draws together many motifs from this area but made a new departure in giving the active lead role to a female character, Ripley, played by Sigourney Weaver. Here the commercial spaceship *Nostromo* encounters a derelict alien craft floating in space. One of the crew explores the vessel and discovers a chamber full of eggs, one of which opens, releasing an organism which attaches itself to his face. Throughout the film, the alien life form is represented in visceral forms, as if it is an organism with intestines, and in a climactic scene a creature bursts from Kane's chest in a travesty birth sequence, where the human host is killed. The alien then escapes into the *Nostromo* and the film builds up a powerful claustrophobia as the crew attempt to track it down. Scott introduced a subsidiary alien theme in revealing that one of the crew members was an android under orders from the 'company' (never named) to bring the alien home. Also, Scott mostly showed the alien organism in part-shots or brief glimpses, keeping its overall appearance a mystery until late into the film. As usual in alien narratives, survival is the paramount issue. Scott originally planned to have Ripley killed, but the studio insisted that she should survive and the alien be killed. The film was released to much acclaim and produced three sequels: *Aliens* (1983), an action adventure on the aliens' home planet; *Alien 3* (1992), describing how an alien egg is unwittingly brought to Earth in a spacecraft which crashes and how Ripley discovers an alien inside her; and *Alien Resurrection* (1997), set in a future when the US Army is planning a programme of cloning starting with Ripley.

By the time Heinlein's *The Puppet Masters* was published, the twin motifs of UFOs and extraterrestrial visitors had been established in SF, although the expression 'Unidentified Flying Object' was not coined until 1952. The supposed crash of a UFO in 1947 near Roswell, New Mexico, followed by an autopsy on an extraterrestrial, has entered popular mythology partly because of the rapid cover-up by the US Army. Whitley Strieber's reportage novel about the incident, *Majestic* (1989), leaves the subject ultimately unproven. The 1950s saw a proliferation of visits by extraterrestrials, usually by means of flying saucers. In *The Day the Earth Stood Still* (1951), an alien, in all respects identical with contemporary humanity except for his unusual dress and technological sophistication, visits the Earth to warn scientists against extending violence into space as they will be stopped by invincible robots. This cautionary tale warns against military escalation in the depths of the Cold War. *Earth vs. the Flying Saucers* (1956) actually showed that escalation when a saucer lands at a US base and an exchange of fire follows, which rapidly grows to a full-scale invasion by the aliens. This film was based on a book on UFOs by Donald Keyhoe, a marine who had been publishing SF stories in the pulps for years.

Steven Spielberg's *Close Encounters of the Third Kind* (1977) revives the motif through lavish and spectacular flying saucers and the representation of the aliens as shorter humanoids. The latter, as a result, do not come across as threatening, especially once communication is established using light effects, tonal musical phrases, and hand signs. The film's title positions its action in the third phase of alien encounter: visual sighting, physical traces, and finally contact. The separation of this process into phases marks how far the motif had come since Murray Leinster's 1945 novella *First Contact*, in which two spaceships meet in space but get caught in an impasse of mutual suspicion, a reaction that was criticized by the Soviet SF novelist Ivan Efremov.

Sympathetic aliens

Signs of the transformation of the alien away from threat can be seen in the 1951 film *The Day the Earth Stood Still*, in which a single humanoid and an accompanying robot come on a mission of goodwill, or in Arthur C. Clarke's 1953 novel *Childhood's End*, in which benign extraterrestrial Overlords take over humanity. Zenna Henderson's People stories, begun in the 1950s, explicitly reject the bug-eyed monster stereotype to explore subtler forms of difference, and treatment of newcomers by local communities. In her stories, alienness is not physically evident, as is the case in Walter Tevis's *The Man Who Fell to Earth* (1963). In the latter, the newcomer is an extraterrestrial, but more a human outsider than an alien being, and as a result subject to interrogation by the CIA and FBI. The absence of hostile intent is explained by his need for help from Earth for his people on another planet. The 1976 film adaptation had David Bowie play the humanoid, but with orange hair, giving a more theatrical dimension to the action.

Clearly, in these examples writers are using the concept of the alien to explore human characteristics, as does the African American novelist Octavia Butler in her Patternist novels, begun in 1976. *Patternmaster* is set in a future when humans are dominated by a network of telepaths. The Patternist sequence presents a secret history of how this group is formed from two prototype immortal characters from late 17th century onwards. *Wild Seed* (1980) describes these beginnings in Africa against a background of slavery and follows Doro (the telepathic male) and Anyanwa (the female shapeshifter and personification of fertility) to the USA, where these characters learn that civilization involves institutionalized suppression of differences. Butler's *Xenogenesis* trilogy (1987–9) focuses on the alien Oankali (with three sexes, permanently exiled from their 'homeworld') attempting to take over humans through gene substitution. The protagonist Lilith comes to consciousness from an artificially induced long sleep to confront a member of the Oankali – grey in colour with ear hair and no nose – who speaks fluently to her. Butler was always conscious of the physicality of her characters, but paces her narrative carefully so that our sense of alien appearance and therefore difference shifts constantly. Butler herself has stated that her books are 'stories of power [...] I bring together multi-racial groups of men and women who must cope with one another's differences as well as with new, not necessarily controllable abilities within themselves'.

Where Butler uses SF to trace out an alternative history of slavery, Orson Scott Card presents a re-imagined version of the colonization of South America in his 1986 novel *Speaker for the Dead*, which is set on the colony of Lusitania in the distant future. The Pequeninos ('little ones' in Spanish) are a native race studied and confined within a fence by their human overlords, and the novel explores the complex difficulties of communication between the two groups. Like Ursula Le Guin's 1976 novel *The Word for World is Forest*, which presents a critique of the Vietnam War through the medium of SF, Card's narrative dramatizes the misunderstandings which arise in power relations between Western and non-literate cultures.

Similarly, Gwyneth Jones's decision to name her own aliens 'Aleutian' shrewdly retains a sense of human remoteness and marginality (the Aleuts have suffered at the hands of both Russians and Americans). She describes the genesis of her *Aleutian Trilogy* (1991–7) as involving a rejection of the Darwinian paradigm of conquer or be conquered. Their own contacts with humans were to be gradual, and they themselves were to embody characteristics of African and Asian cultures while at the same time being sexless humanoids. In her own terms, the Aleutians were modelled as 'women' and 'native peoples', and displayed a scepticism towards spoken language. She chose the latter because 'words divide', but of necessity had to represent the Aleutians' silent empathetic communication on the page as similar to human speech within non-standard speech marks. The result was that she realized she had 'made the Aleutians very like feminist women in all this: creatures dead set on *having it all*, determined to be self-aware and articulate public people, without giving up their place in the natural world'.

The 1988 film *Alien Nation* returns the alien theme to the US domestic question of race. After a pastiche opening sequence of a huge saucer landing in the Mohave Desert, we are told by a newsreader that it brought thousands of humanoids, who were genetically designed for slave labour. The Newcomers, as they become known, settle in Los Angeles and San Francisco. Unusually for this subgenre, the film shows how the Newcomers are being treated three years after their arrival. Through the pattern of a cop-and-partner crime investigation, they are shown to be the new underclass, derided and shunned by Chinese American, African American, and Latino characters alike.

7. **Still from Graham Baker's *Alien Nation* (1988)**

In other words, the alien invasion is used to make a comment on racism and assimilation through the developing relationship between the alienated white cop Sykes and his partner the Newcomer Francisco. The theme is handled with relative ease because the Newcomers have altered heads, which tempts the viewer to think they are all the same, but otherwise visually similar to humans. The film's title has been used in two later publications, both called *Alien Nation*. Peter Brimelow's 1995 volume attacks US immigration policy for encouraging migration from the developing world, and Cannon Schmidt's study of 1997 discusses the ethnic subtext to 19th-century Gothic fiction.

Language

The clichéd image of an alien emerging from a flying saucer and declaring 'Take me to your leader' highlights one problem in alien narratives. As soon as aliens speak, their otherness becomes compromised, because we associate language with a way of life and view it as one of the defining characteristics of humanity. One way out of this impasse in early SF was to use the convenience of an instant translation device. Or telepathy might come into play. In Edwin Lester Arnold's *Lieutenant Gulliver Jones* (1905), the hero learns Martian by telepathic projection.

When novelists began to address the problem of other languages, they tended to draw on the Sapir-Whorf hypothesis that our worldview is shaped by our language and also to show how language could be caught up in power play. Suzette Haden Elgin's *Native Tongue* series (1984) presents a future world where Linguists (male) reign over an inter-planetary empire in a regime within which women are reduced to total subservience. The title refers to a communal composition of their own language by the women of a particular household. Since this is forbidden, the composition becomes an act of collective enabling as well as resistance. The resulting language of Laadan, which Elgin hoped to promote, is given in a sampler appendix. A professional linguist herself, Elgin insists in *The Language Imperative* (2000) that language can't be owned, simply practised.

Michael Bishop has taken a more anthropological approach in his *Transfigurations* (1979), which contains 'Death and Designation Among the Asadi' and 'Sundry Notes for an Abortive Ethnography'. There is a strong analogy in the novel between Kenya and the planet of BoskVelt (Bosky Veldt), where the protagonist goes to study the Asadi. He keeps a journal, but data are always outstripping his hypotheses, so that ultimately any rational report is impossible. Bishop's novel thus contrasts strongly with Ursula Le Guin's *Always Coming Home* (1985), which clearly grows out of her family grounding in anthropology. Indeed, the novel is partly modelled on an anthropological report, complete with appendices and glossary. It opens with the narrator investigating the 'archaeology of the future', when Pandora is trying to open the 'box' of Kesh culture in northern California. Through graphics, recorded oral tales, and so on we are constantly reminded of the text's mediation of a hybrid culture, which takes forms and values from pre-industrial Nature but also uses electronic connections with the outside world which collectively constitute a cybernetic 'City of the Mind'.

Since the 1970s, the concept of the alien has become assimilated increasingly into cultural debates about gender and ethnicity, with the result that the old-style invader from space has tended to recede from SF, except for works like Whitley Strieber's non-fictional accounts of perceived extraterrestrial visitations. The appearance of aliens has constantly shifted too according to different perceptions of race and species. The famous Klingons from the *Star Trek* series were originally shown as possessing darker complexions, then later given more elaborate physical differences. An extensive Klingon language was even devised by Marc Okrand which subsequently has attracted its own cult following. A further reason for the attenuation of the alien may be that its treatment has become increasingly caught up in technological systems, to which we now turn.

Chapter 3
Science fiction and technology

Partly for historical reasons to do with its self-promotion in the early 20th century, science fiction is popularly associated with the evolution of technology, by which is usually meant tools or implements. However, the American cultural historian Lewis Mumford's notion of 'technics' is more helpful because it is broader and includes information transfer. One of the most recurrent themes in science fiction is its examination of humanity's relation to its own material constructions, sometimes to celebrate progress, sometimes in a more negative spirit of what Isaac Asimov has repeatedly described as technophobia, through fictions articulating fears of human displacement. As we shall see later in this chapter, the city becomes a key embodiment of futuristic technology and, as the German sociologist Walter Benjamin showed, a labyrinthine, fragmented space, which encouraged characteristically urban processes of cognition on its inhabitants.

Technology is a central indicator of change in science fiction. Indeed, in his history of SF, Roger Luckhurst defines the fiction as a 'literature of technologically saturated societies', and he proceeds to trace out this tradition from the late 19th century up to the present. The pioneering efforts by the Luxembourg-born SF writer and editor Hugo Gernsback to make technology central to this fiction were partly systematizing the myriad references to technological innovations which filled science fiction at the turn of the century: references to the telegraph and visual means of information transfer, the first applications of electricity, flying machines, new military weapons, and anti-gravity devices. The latter began to appear in narratives of space flight, usually in a perfunctory form, but at least the writers realized the need to provide a token explanation of how travel through space was possible.

Gernsback, Campbell, and 'hard' science fiction

The very phrase 'science fiction' suggests a combination of non-fiction and fiction such as we find in the writings of Hugo Gernsback. His most famous novel *Ralph 124C 41+* ('one to foresee for one'), serialized in 1911, published as a book in 1925, articulates his conviction that the new fiction should contain instruction in science as well as entertainment. Ralph himself is introduced through his laboratory, the place of invention, and the world of 2660 emerges as one characterized by its new technological wonders: devices like the 'telephot' (a form of television), ultra-short radio waves, and the 'hypnobioscope', a device for transmitting information directly to the brain, later satirized in *Brave New World*. As Gary Westfahl has shown, Gernsback lacked skill in combining science and fiction, as a result sometimes showing these elements serially and describing Ralph in double terms as the inventive scientist *and* the melodramatic hero who could protect the heroine from the unscrupulous villain. Nevertheless, Gernsback pioneered the presentation of the modern technologized environment. As Ralph and the heroine skate down Broadway one evening on their 'tele-motor-coasters', New York seems to be the ultimate city of light, the ultimate electrified city, for the novel celebrates electricity throughout, as had the Chicago World's Fair in 1893. It is no coincidence that in 1908 Gernsback founded the magazine *Modern Electrics*, the first of its kind.

His use of neologisms also set a trend which was to be developed in later SF. Two of the most famous are 'robot', coined by the Czech writer Karel Capek in 1920, or 'cyberspace' from the American writer William Gibson in 1982, the latter used to describe the virtual space of cumulative computer networks. In these cases, the terms have taken on a broader currency beyond literature, but the use of neologisms has been explained by the critic Marc Angenot. Marc Angenot has shown that such neologisms cue in a conjectural reading of SF texts where we construct a context for such terms and thereby also the virtual world of such narratives.

Gernsback placed technical innovation in the foreground of his novel because he closely identified technology with the general progress of humanity. This meant that in his SF magazines he favoured those stories which celebrated science. In an editorial for 1931, 'Wonders of the Machine Age', he stated his avowed policy of not accepting stories which attributed the evils of the time to technology and which foresaw great concentrations of wealth where an oligarchy would use their industrial might to enslave humanity. He vowed to reject 'propaganda of this sort which tends to inflame an unreasoning public against scientific progress, against useful machines, and against inventions in general'. By playing down the industrial organization needed to produce and distribute the inventions he describes, Gernsback here set his face against an increasing current of suspicion towards technology which was gathering head in the 1930s. Later in the century, in 1978, another SF writer heavily committed to the cause of science education, Isaac Asimov, surveyed the treatment of technology in science fiction, identifying two strands of development – one optimistic (with which he identified) and one expressing the fear that machines may get out of control. The 'Myth of the Machine', as he called it, was a double-edged concept reflected in the frequent suspicions of the applications of technology in much subsequent science fiction.

The fiction following in the tradition of Gernsback and John W. Campbell, the editor of *Astounding Science Fiction* from 1937 onwards, became known from the 1950s as 'hard' science fiction, as distinct from 'soft' SF, which deals with social issues. Campbell's trenchant editorial policy promoted the incorporation of technology into the fiction of his discoveries, figures like Robert Heinlein, A. E. Van Vogt, and Isaac Asimov, whose collective writing around the period of the Second World War is sometimes referred to as the golden age of science fiction. Campbell's powerful influence, however, should not be seen as prescriptive or restrictive, more of a steady pressure on his authors to produce professional narratives, a pressure particularly evident in US science fiction from the 1950s onwards, from the decade which saw the development of cybernetics pioneered by Norbert Wiener. A key concept in this emerging discipline was the analogy with, not opposition between, humans and machines.

In the introduction to his 1994 anthology of hard science fiction, David G. Hartwell spells out some of the characteristics of these novels. For him, they combine a concern with scientific truth with a conservatism of method and a general suspicion of the literary. Nevertheless, they have their own tensions, especially between the distance of the narratives from the real world and their simultaneous appeal to real-world scientific principles. Although he doesn't spell it out as such, he implies a certain optimism of vision in these works, which embody the 'fantasies of empowerment of the scientific and technological culture of the modern era'. Key practitioners of science fiction tied closely to scientific concepts are the Australian Greg Egan, Stephen Baxter in Britain, and in the USA Vernor Vinge and Rudy Rucker, both academic mathematicians.

The novel which is often presented as the supreme example of hard SF is Hal Clement's *Mission of Gravity* (1954), which describes the exploration of an obloid planet named Mesklin. The novel presents an impressive example of world-building in which every aspect of the new planet is rendered as scientifically self-consistent. The narrative describes a series of essentially practical problems, such as that of navigation, with their equally practical solutions. When he turns his attention to the planet-dwellers, Clement is more cautious. Despite some physical differences, the Mesklinites come across as proxy humans with their own point of view, not least because they converse with the Earthlings in faultless English.

In contrast, a novel which would question the nature of empowerment is Joe Haldeman's *The Forever War* (1974), a military *Bildungsroman* in which the author transposes his experiences in Vietnam on to outer space. The novel powerfully dramatizes the ambivalence of the narrator Mandella towards the interstellar war against the 'Taurans', creatures hardly ever seen, of puzzling appearance, sometimes even mistaken for animals. Mandella receives training in sophisticated weaponry which includes post-hypnotic suggestion before battle. As a result of this conditioning, he develops a nightmare sense of himself dehumanized into a fighting machine. Haldeman evokes danger, but more from the extraterrestrial situation and the unreliability of the soldiers' equipment than from the supposed enemy. The novel makes ironic use of the conventions of star wars to evoke the timelessness of a war without obvious goals, the self-contradictions of the military training, and to present the whole enterprise as a form of latter-day colonialism.

One of the leading current practitioners of hard SF is Jerry Pournelle, who has written a number of military narratives and who could be seen as the heir to Robert Heinlein's patriotism, with the difference that Pournelle has been closely involved with the US military establishment over the years. In contrast with Haldeman, he has represented the colonization of space as a logical continuation of the American frontier, and in his 1970 political study *The Strategy of Technology* (written with Stefan T. Possony) argues that since at least 1945 the USA has been engaged in a technological war against the Soviet Union. This political imperative informs Pournelle's treatment of fictional themes relating to space, and in 1981 he became chair of the Citizens'

Advisory Council on National Space Policy, whose membership included Robert Heinlein and Gregory Benford. This Council helped formulate President Reagan's Strategic Defence Initiative (SDI), popularly known as Star Wars.

Even here, however, it would be a gross simplification to suggest that Pournelle celebrates technological progress. One of his most powerful novels, co-written with Larry Niven, *Oath of Fealty* (1982), examines the working of an 'arcology', a term coined by the architect Paolo Soleri by combining 'architecture' with 'ecology'. Although a neologism, the term suggests the massive residential complexes we find in Wells and other authors. In *Oath of Fealty*, following a race riot on the edge of near-future Los Angeles, a huge self-supporting community has been built named Todos Santos ('All Saints') which houses a quarter of a million residents. The complex has been built with private capital and appears to be self-sufficient, with its own security system, but the deaths of two youngsters who infiltrate an accessway demonstrate that Todos Santos actually depends on the nearby city, and here one of the strengths of the novel comes out. It not only depicts an arcology but characters argue over its social value; one unflattering analogy is with a termite hill. Similarly, the novel contains many references to science fiction as embodying the pool of ideas which produced the complex. The shopping mall contains moving walkways, whose prototype is acknowledged in the text to belong to Heinlein. In short, *Oath of Fealty* simultaneously presents a technological innovation and debates it throughout.

The city

The city is the supreme embodiment of technological construction, and for this reason science fiction has been a heavily urban literary mode. Even Richard Jefferies' *After London* (1885), which is a post-urban narrative describing the restoration of Nature after London has sunk into a fetid bog, could be read as a protest against 19th-century developments of the city. The different

MAISON TOURNANTE AÉRIENNE

8. Aerial rotating house from Albert Robida's *Le Vingtième Siècle* (1890)

renderings of the city in science fiction use it as a laboratory for technological change. Albert Robida's *Le Vingtième Siècle* (*The Twentieth Century*, 1890), for example, describes the transformation of Paris in the near future. It is a comic vision of commercialism run rampant. One illustration shows the Arc de Triomphe after it has been bought by speculators, where a massive iron platform dwarfs the arch and supports the new International Hotel, built in a hybrid style to be as imposing as possible. The visual imbalance comments comically on the new priorities of the 20th century, reflected also in the proliferation of advertising signs and the preoccupation with rapid transport. There is even an electric tramway in the Louvre to speed visitors past the exhibits without fatigue. The 'aerial rotating house' shows the elevated position of new inventions above the conventional city. Robida's is a city of metal, of ubiquitous ironwork.

Fritz Lang's *Metropolis* (1927, reissued 2002) supplied the prototype image of the city in science fiction film. It was strictly speaking two images: Metropolis above ground, the level for the managing elite and their families, and the Workers' City underground. The opening title sequence gives complete priority to setting, to the stepped complex of the master, modelled partly on Brueghel's *Tower of Babel* and partly on Lang's impressions of Manhattan, which dissolves into shots of huge machines in operation.

It is these machines which define Metropolis as an urban-industrial complex with a monstrous life of its own. In her original 1927 novel, Thea von Harbou describes the uniform dress and movement of the workers in this 'New Tower of Babel', an effect repeated in the film through the structural hierarchy of Metropolis, which places the workers even under the machines. *Metropolis* set a pattern of imagery for subsequent science fiction portrayals of the city, a pattern that relates closely to urban planning of the 1920s, such as the architect Hugh Ferriss's *The*

9. Still from Fritz Lang's *Metropolis* (1927)

Metropolis of Tomorrow (1929) which applies modernist, geometrical shapes to city planning.

At the end of *A Modern Utopia* (1905), H. G. Wells describes the shock of his protagonist returning to London from the wholesome spaces and cleanliness of his Swiss-type utopia. Suddenly his surroundings are packed with jostling, often misshapen townsfolk. He suffers from a kind of sensory overload through sight, hearing, and smell. It is exactly this sort of disorder which Wells tries to avoid in his futuristic cities, not always for the better. In *When the Sleeper Wakes* (1899), Graham finds himself totally estranged from London some two centuries into the future. He is told that 'today is the day of wealth' and the physical expression of this wealth is the city's 'Titanic buildings'. Although the city where he finds himself is still London, it is so radically transformed that it has become unrecognizable, and Wells increases this effect of urban estrangement by including only a minimum of place names. In the film *Things To Come* (1936), made by Alexander Korda with Wells's collaboration, the transition from imminent present into the 21st century is made through changes to Everytown, Wells's representative city, through war to reconstruction. The opening of the film makes it clear that Everytown initially is based on London, as the 1930 film of an urban future, *Just Imagine*, uses New York. In the latter, the city of 1980 has become a spectacular metropolis of huge high-rise buildings and air and road traffic at different levels. Similarly, *Things To Come* shows a streamlined underground city whose architectural lines, as Wells intended, are 'bold and colossal'. The overwhelming impression of size is achieved by dwarfing the human figures at the bottom of frames, which has the effect of making them seem anonymous functionaries, there to reveal the new sublime architecture of the industrial city. Indeed, the first signs of life in the city are industrial activities.

The city in Wells and in *Metropolis* is an emblem of industrial order. In the same way, *The City of Endless Night* (1920), by the American nutritionist Milo Hastings, describes a world of the future where Germany rules thanks to its invention of a death ray. The control centre of this regime is a new underground Berlin, a massive urban-industrial complex housing millions which represents the culmination for the American narrator of the application of science to society. Its enormous mess halls and factories present him with an 'atmosphere of perfect order, perfect system, perfect discipline', whose excessive order makes the city inhuman.

Cities have regularly been used to embody dystopian futures. Clifford D. Simak's *City* (a 1952 'fix-up' of stories linked by an editorial commentary), situates its present in the future when both cities and humanity itself have died out. The tales are narrated as legends by dogs who give an ironic external perspective on whether humans or cities ever existed at all. In the preamble, we are told that a city seems to be an 'impossible structure', unbelievably confining for a supposedly rational creature to live in. James Blish's *Cities in Flight* weaves one of the most unusual variations on this theme by showing cities as spaceships. *A Life for the Stars* (1962) describes the situation which make these urban space rovers necessary. As raw materials have become exhausted, people 'go Okie' (the slang name of the migrants in *The Grapes of Wrath*), leaving their land to hunt for work. Blish presents a latter-day Depression where the cities in space embody different social possibilities. John Brunner's *The Squares of the City* (1965) explores the connections between a rectangular layout, open spaces, and political control in his South American capital city Vados. Harry Harrison's *Make Room! Make Room!* (1966) is set in New York of 1999, a symptomatic representation of the world's over-population where the food supply has become critical. The 1973 movie adaptation took as its title *Soylent Green*, the name of a synthetic food wafer. Finally, Philip Wylie's *Los Angeles: AD 2017* (1971) describes a future city where severe pollution has driven life underground. In these and similar novels, crisis brings about a fascistic administration.

One of the most complex and surreal depictions of a city is given in Samuel Delany's *Dhalgren* (1975), in which disaster has struck the city of Bellona (named after the Roman goddess of war). The protagonist drifts into the city, has brief sexual encounters, meets gangs and other survivors, but never develops any overall sense of the city layout. Delany manages this effect by keeping the narrative perspective close to the protagonist's perceptions. So, however many blocks he crosses, however many derelict buildings he clambers through, he never develops any sense of distance. Space and time shift constantly, as does his visual perception of the city, which is obscured by the smoke from random fires. Delany maintains an austerely consistent perspective which never allows the reader to understand more than his protagonist 'Kid', although the narrative intermittently shifts into the third person. The result is a surreal stream of locally vivid episodes within an urban space of uncertain extent. Delany's city is fragmented and ultimately unknowable.

As Vivian Sobchack has argued, post-war SF films tended to show negative images of the city, presenting scenarios either of destruction or of emptying. One sign of this emphasis is the evocation of the city as a control network. So the British television film *Max Headroom* describes the promotion of subliminal programming and *Brazil* (both 1985) shows an Orwellian regime of bureaucratic regulation. Jean-Luc Godard's *Alphaville* (1965) combines three genres: the American private eye story, the spy thriller, and science fiction. The agent Lemmy Caution has come from 'Nueva York' on a mission to capture or kill Professor Von Braun, not the rocket technician we would expect but the designer of a set of computers which include Alpha 60 at the centre of the city in the film, a sort of futuristic Paris. Described as the 'capital city of a distant galaxy', it is the computer itself which interrogates Lemmy once he is arrested.

Ridley Scott's *Blade Runner* (1982) still presents one of the most complex and textured visual renderings of the city of the future. Moving the location from Philip K. Dick's original San Francisco to Los Angeles was strategic because LA has always represented in the American imagination the ultimate city of change. Although the film was set 40 years into the future, the décor also contained countless details of the USA 40 years earlier, that is, of the period of Raymond Chandler and film noir. Scott's habit of 'pictorial referencing' resulted in a unique blend of futuristic and period detail. One moment we see flying cars; the next a series of bicycles run past. The result is that, unusually, we see a future city with a history. Although he didn't live to see the final film, Dick did visit the studios and saw a television report of one shooting session, being impressed by the concrete detail of the method, and declaring: 'It's a world that people actually live in.' The film embodies power in the huge pyramid of the Tyrell Corporation and in the opening sequences uses the central image of an enlarged eye, suggesting at once surveillance, the activities of the blade runner himself as a latter-day private eye, and the only organ which can supposedly distinguish human from replicant.

Robots and cyborgs

The term 'robot' entered the language in 1920 from the Czech writer Karel Capek's play *R.U.R.: Rossum's Universal Robots*, in which the word carried suggestions of heavy labour, even of slavery. As the application of the term developed, it came to mean a self-contained, maybe remote-controlled 'artificial device that mimics the actions and, possibly, the appearance of a human being'. Prior to 1920, the existence of robot-like constructions stretches back to antiquity, devices known as automata or androids (literally, 'man-like'). They begin to appear in 19th-century literature with the dancing automaton in E. T. A. Hoffmann's story 'The Sandman', in Edgar Allen Poe's fascinated comments on Johann Maelzel's chess-playing device, and in Edward Bulwer-Lytton's *The Coming Race* (1871), in which the household of the future includes domestic automata. The first detailed account of such a construction occurs in Edward S. Ellis's *The Huge Hunter or, The Steam Man of the Prairies* (1865), in which the machine is ten feet tall and constructed entirely of iron, and a boiler is housed in its body. By modern standards, it is a crude enough figure, even wearing the 'stove-pipe hat' of the Victorian gentleman. Ellis's machine was steam-driven and combined

10. Illustration to Edward S. Ellis's *The Steam Man of the Prairies* (1865)

elements of locomotion (motive power), humanity (shape), and horse (it was directed by reins).

Once robots begin to appear in 20th-century writing, a number of central issues become apparent. Sidney Fowler Wright's 1929 story 'Automata' evokes a grim future when the automata have superseded humans in a 'triumph' of evolution. In *Metropolis*, the inventor Rotwang constructs a replicant of the character Maria. And in *R.U.R.*, the robots take over the world economy. Displacement and replication become two of the main fears in robot narratives, fears of humans losing their centrality. Philip K. Dick's *Do Androids Dream of Electric Sheep?* (1968), the original novel on which *Blade Runner* was based, makes the second of these fears into its central subject. Organic androids have been designed to work in the Martian colonies but have fled that chattel slavery to come to a ruined Earth following World War

Terminus. In his pursuit of these for the San Francisco Police Department, Rick Deckard constantly questions the nature of identity. The novel shows from the very first page a world already mechanized in many respects, and even the state religion, Mercerism, is named after an industrial method for treating fabrics. How then to distinguish replicants from human originals? Deckard has no answer to this and even demonstrates a reluctance to believe that all replicants are non-human. Similarly, in the third act of *R.U.R.* two robots begin to demonstrate human feelings, and so perhaps we should add a third fear to robots: that they might make it ultimately impossible to identify humans.

The writer who has promoted a consistently positive vision of robots is Isaac Asimov, who began publishing his robot stories in the 1940s and who, in a bid to combat technophobia – what he called the 'Frankenstein complex' – formulated his famous Three Laws of Robotics:

1) A robot may not injure a human being or, through inaction, allow a human being to come to harm.
2) A robot must obey any orders given to it by human beings, except where such orders would conflict with the First Law.
3) A robot must protect its own existence as long as such protection does not conflict with the First or Second Law.

Asimov's simple strategy of describing robots rationally and 'as machines rather than metaphors' transformed their representation in science fiction. Apart from his commitment to technological representation, Asimov also extends the trope of robots as workers. 'The Bicentennial Man' (1976) is a particularly interesting example for its implicit treatment of race. In common with many of Asimov's later robot stories, the opening humanizes the subject as Andrew Martin, delaying the reader's recognition that he is a robot. Only the 'smooth blankness' of his face gives us a hint. Throughout this story, there is a running analogy between the robot and an African American; thus the ending, when Andrew strives for recognition as a man, is loaded with racial as well as humanistic significance, especially given the circumstances of the story's publication during the national Bicentennial year.

Although the dividing line between the two is not hard and fast, the cyborg is different from a robot in being a hybrid creation. Coined in 1960 in relation to survival in outer space, a cyborg is a cybernetic organism, crudely a combination of human and machine. Martin Caidin's 1972 novel *Cyborg* describes how a pilot, grotesquely injured in a crash, has his body reconstructed by the secret government Office of Strategic Operations on condition that he works for them. The narrative extrapolates one of the most common applications of cybernetic organisms, namely in the field of medicine, and applies it to contemporary power structures. Similarly and more famously, in the 1987 film *RoboCop* a Detroit policeman is reconstructed by Omni Consumer Products, who have taken over the control of the city police force, and released on to the streets as a RoboCop, the ultimate irresistible law-enforcement officer imaged as a kind of armoured cowboy.

11. **Still from Paul Verhoeven's *RoboCop* (1987)**

Here, however, the experiment goes wrong. Although it doesn't produce a cyborg, *Frankenstein* sets the narrative paradigm. The RoboCop's original memory has not been erased, and the second half of the film follows his attempts to get revenge on his 'killers'.

The best-known film treatment of the cyborg is the *Terminator* series starring Arnold Schwarzenegger. In the launch film, the action is set in the present (1984) with two irruptions from the future of 2029: the Terminator and his antagonist. The Terminator is an armoured killing machine on the inside covered by a layer of living human tissue. He is, in other words, a cybernetic assassin, who for Donna Haraway, because of his capacity to repair himself, represents the 'self-sufficient, self-generated Tool in all of its infinite but self-identical variations'. It also breaks a mould for action movies in showing the Terminator's defeat at the hands of his intended female victim.

Donna Haraway has produced the major theorization of the cyborg in her 1985 essay 'A Cyborg Manifesto', in which she deploys the concept as a polemical tool for breaking down spuriously sharp distinctions like that between human and machine. Drawing on feminist SF by Joanna Russ and others, she gives the cyborg a cultural centrality as representing the hybrid nature of our contemporary existence and argues that Rachel, the replicant in *Blade Runner* simultaneously desired and feared by Rick Deckard, is the 'image of a cyborg culture's fear, love, and confusion'.

Haraway's use of the cyborg to examine social and sexual issues was followed in Marge Piercy's 1991 novel *He, She and It* (*Body of Glass* outside the USA), set in a Jewish enclave within the America of 2059. An illegal cyborg named Yod (the tenth letter of the Hebrew alphabet) has been created to protect the settlement just as, according to legend, the Golem was created out of clay in the 16th century to protect the Jewish community of Prague. Piercy alternates chapters recapitulating the Golem story with those tracing the evolving relationship between Yod and the protagonist Shira. The alienness of the cyborg is radically reduced by 'his' capacity to engage in reflection, register pleasure, and even identify his own tradition as a 'monster'. Yod's allusion to *Frankenstein* implies that his creation is a kind of birthing. In fact, he comes across less as a hybrid creature, since his mechanism is largely unseen, than an ideally rational being who does not possess taboos.

The construction of robots and cyborgs in the human image suggests that technology frequently operates in science fiction to dissect or disassemble the body for purposes of reconstruction and modification. Critics like J. P. Telotte argue that this is *the* technological theme in SF, dating back of course to *Frankenstein*, which Brian Aldiss and others have taken as the proto-text of science fiction. The ambivalence of this text towards experimentation is suggested in the way Frankenstein violates taboos of respect to construct a person out of dead parts and in the fact that the 'monster' (or 'daemon' as he is called) has no name and therefore cannot be perceived in separation from Frankenstein. The switches of perspective between creator and created only reinforce this effect. In early SF narratives of biological engineering, this duality between experimenter and subject recurs, ultimately with fatal results for the former: Jekyll and Hyde, Wells's Dr Moreau and his Beast People, the surgeons and Harry Benson in Michael Crichton's *The Terminal Man* (1972). In the last of these, implanted electrodes are controlled by a nearby computer, implying that Benson can only receive therapy by sacrificing his autonomy. As implants increased in sophistication, so did the imagination of how the self could be modified. One of the most paranoid possibilities is shown in the 1990 film *Total Recall* (based on a story by Philip K. Dick), in which implanted memories have become commodified as a kind of virtual tourism. However, when Douglas Quaid visits the Rekall company for 'treatment', it is discovered that he has already had his memory erased. From that point on, his identity splinters into

64

two when he receives a video image from Hauser, his other self, and when he enters Mars disguised as a woman. Right to the very end, he proves unable to find any definite verification of his self.

Computers

The very term 'computer' carries a double meaning which is reflected in its presentations in science fiction. The word could denote a person who makes calculations or a machine doing similar operations, and the question that has recurred throughout post-war SF on computers is: do they facilitate or entrap? Do they help or displace human activity? The prevalence of fictional views seems to come out on the second of these possibilities. Kurt Vonnegut's first novel *Player Piano* (1952) describes the use by the US government of EPICAC XIV, a giant computer which predicts how many commodities will be needed by the citizens. Prediction, however, has become prescription, and the computer determines the most efficient way for work to be performed, regardless of how many people lose employment as a result. For Vonnegut, the computer reflects and reinforces a mechanization of behaviour, speech, and even thought.

Philip K. Dick's 1960 novel *Vulcan's Hammer* raises the more paranoid possibility of surveillance by his own super-computer named Vulcan. This is housed beneath Geneva, at the heart of the world government, and generates mobile electronic units which circulate, gathering information about their subjects. Ira Levin's *This Perfect Day* (1970) elaborates on these themes in a more explicitly dystopian way. Once again, we have a world state, this time presided over by the computer UniComp, which assigns names to children and dispatches 'advisers' who are called in whenever an individual displays unorthodox behaviour. Behind the computer there lies a hidden elite of programmers, who are dedicated, like the bureaucrats in *Nineteen Eighty-Four*, to maintaining the status quo indefinitely.

Computers have been related to the military since Bernard Wolfe's *Limbo* (1952), which explores the perverse roots of aggression during the Cold War. The military establishments of East and West have both become computerized, with the result that both sides now possess 'cyberneticized militaries'. Once again, displacement occurs and the two computers mirror each other's activities in sending personnel to different confrontation points around the world. A similar mirroring operates in Mordecai Roshwald's *Level 7* (1959), in which the narrator is an operative in a mechanized underground defence bunker and nuclear war is triggered by the automatic instruction for him to push the button. Wolfe's is a very early treatment of essentially the same scenario described in Mack Reynolds's *Computer War* (1967), where the world is divided into two states, Alphaland and Betastan. Only Alphaland possesses a computer, which predicts the economic superiority of that regime over its rival and the inevitability of world rule. However, the second country's behaviour repeatedly contradicts these predictions, which remain unfulfilled. The symbolic presence of computers in the political oppositions of the Cold War is also demonstrated in *Giles Goat-Boy* (1966) by John Barth, not known primarily as a writer of SF. Here, the West is shown as an enormous university campus presided over by a computer called WESCAC, which has gradually taken over all areas of decision-making and which demonstrates that the new political currency is information. WESCAC is paralleled in the other campus (i.e. in the East) by EASCAC, and in a confrontation which reads like an allegory of East and West Berlin, it is suggested hypothetically that the boundaries drawn by the computers are completely arbitrary.

The predominant emphasis in these novels is to show how computers are used to support a corrupt power system. As they approach sentience or as they are anthropomorphized, this identification with autocracy becomes all the easier. Robert Heinlein's *The Moon is a Harsh Mistress* (1966) seems to fit this pattern, though developments in the novel suggest a more complex situation is evolving. Heinlein gives us a parable on colonialism where the Moon has become a convenient dumping ground for criminals and other 'undesirables'. The authorities use a computer, HOLMES IV, to administer these colonies, and the plot begins with the computer beginning to behave anomalously. The narrator is Manuel, or 'Man', a computer programmer, who refers to the computer as 'Mike', not only a humanizing move but one which associates the computer with rational analysis through references to Mycroft, Sherlock Holmes's brother. As the novel develops, 'Mike' seems to come progressively alive, devising a pseudonym and facial appearance for itself, and using an increasingly sophisticated idiom of 'speech'. Far from supporting the commercial/imperial regime, 'Mike' becomes a leading player in the Moon's revolution against its brutal masters.

Up to the 1970s, computers were shown to be large console banks with a definite location. In the wake of miniaturization and the proliferation of electronic systems, computers tend to recede from SF as objects and to be assimilated into complex systems for the circulation of information. As they took on increasing sophistication, computers tended to become assimilated into a totalizing electronic environment. The 1999 film *The Matrix* embodies this transition in its presentation of reality as an elaborate electronic simulation to blind individuals to the 'truth'. The protagonist Thomas Anderson is described as an official computer programmer but also a secret hacker. He learns that an extended struggle is taking place between humans and machines some time in the future. In fact, much of the film's power grows out of the ways in which it destabilizes these polarities of truth/illusion, public/private, and human/machine. The repeated breaking of frames makes it impossible for the viewer to locate any unmediated reality, and in this respect we are well on the way to a contemporary presentation of the Internet as an electronic expanse with no centre and no controlling intelligence. *The Matrix* and its sequels also demonstrate the interpenetration of information technology and the body signalled in the double meaning of the title which indicates an electronic network and draws on its etymological meaning of 'womb'. Thus the protagonist's body moves with the dictates of plot and intermittently becomes the site of that plot, in short becomes itself technologized.

Cyberpunk and after

Cyberpunk fiction emerged in the 1980s, partly in response to the 'tools of global integration', as Bruce Sterling puts it in his introduction to *Mirrorshades: The Cyberpunk Anthology* (1986). For Sterling, it was a fiction of globalization: 'Cyberpunk has little patience with borders', he declares. Valuable as his emphasis is, the complex incorporation of technology was one of the hallmarks of this fiction, as can be seen in William Gibson's *Neuromancer* (1984), in which the term 'cyberspace' was coined. Later applications interpret it as denoting the data in a network imaged through a three-dimensional model or more loosely as a body of information within a set of systems represented as an open environment without limit. The second of these gives us the more helpful access to *Neuromancer*, which combines aspects of noir crime fiction with new images of computing activity. The novel combines two plot lines: the relation between Case, the protagonist, and Molly (the 'new romance' in the title), and Case's search for a means to remove toxins from his system. This last term is used deliberately because what gives the novel its complexity of plot is the sheer proliferation of systems at every level, from the body through criminal networks to the matrix. The opening scene takes place in a bar where the barman has a prosthetic arm and steel teeth. This sets a keynote for the novel in that every character seems to be in some sense either a cyborg or the recipient of invasive measures like the corruption of Case's nervous system with toxins. The latter almost immobilize him and reduce him to dreaming of the matrix, remembering his days as a computer hacker. He forms a relationship with Molly, a streetwise character with surgically inset glasses and with retractable deadly blades at the ends of her fingers. These and other characters move through the Sprawl, a composite term for a conurbation, whether in Japan, the USA, or Turkey. Despite the nominal differences between these locations, Gibson's globalism emerges in his evocation of a worldwide system of corporate power which represents the working of late capitalism. Just as characters have been 'invaded' by prosthetics, drugs, or electronic data, so they act within a world where every aspect of the environment seems to have suffered imaging through the matrix, holograms, or genetic engineering. In that sense, Gibson evokes a totally technologized world figured through tropes like that of the lattice, whereby everything becomes flattened out as data to be processed.

This same impetus is central to *Pattern Recognition* (2003), a novel in which Gibson situates the action in the present – not a major change since he has repeatedly insisted that SF interprets the present, not the future. As the title suggests, the novel describes attempts by Cayce (a female revision of Case) to locate the origins of mysterious video clips posted on the Internet. The very notion of origin is problematic in a global network which can be accessed anywhere, and interpretation itself – the novel's central subject – is complicated by processes of steganography and encryption.

Whereas Gibson hints in *Pattern Recognition* that the Russian Mafia might be involved in the videos, his emphasis falls mainly on hermeneutics, on the problem of interpreting data. In contrast, Pat Cadigan's fiction projects a sharper sense of the ownership and regulation of cyber-technology. Her first novel, *Mindplayers* (1987), shows the protagonist Allie finding herself on the wrong side of the law by stealing a 'madcap' (a virtual-reality, or VR, helmet), after which she is exhaustively photographed ('everything inside and out') by the Brain Police. This Orwellian organization gives 'dry-cleaning' the sinister connotations of brainwashing, but marks a development beyond *Nineteen Eighty-Four* in the sophistication of the enforcement technology. Now physical acts like strip-searching are internal, suggesting that minds are state property. *Synners* (1991) accesses Los Angeles through its media, not only film and video systems but an automated traffic-control network called GridLid. Haunting the city is the fearful expectation of disaster, the 'big one' which might be an earthquake but which in the novel is actually electronic. A general blackout freezes the city in a massive gridlock, which, like everything else there, becomes converted into a media spectacle. Cadigan shares the vision of *Blade Runner* and other works that the city is presided over by a massive, computer-driven entertainment colossus called Diversifications Inc. The image of wiring becomes a powerful articulation not only of individuals' VR experiences but also of a self-expanding network of connections. The 'syn' in the novel's title suggests exactly this connectedness and synthetic dimension to Angelenos' collective experience. Expansion is a commercial fact of life in *Synners*, whereas in Cadigan's 2000 novel *Dervish Is Digital* regulation has become institutionalized. Here, the protagonist is chief officer for the Artificial Reality Division of TechnoCrime, pursuing a VR investigation. Cadigan's narratives significantly revise what some feminist critics found to be a weakness in cyberpunk fiction, namely that it powerfully dramatized the technological penetration of everyday life while leaving unexamined masculinist presumptions of action and style.

Another formative figure in cyberpunk, Neal Stephenson, has explained the title of his 1992 novel *Snow Crash* to mean electron collapse like the loss of image on a TV screen, but it also carries connotations of a come-down after taking cocaine. Snow Crash within the novel thus straddles a metaphor in being at one and the same time a drug and a computer virus. The novel is set in a post-national future where the USA has collapsed into small self-contained enclaves called 'burbclaves'. Hiro, the protagonist, is a computer hacker and pizza delivery boy, in other words, a deliverer of one sort of commodity or another, similar to the courier protagonist of Gibson's *Virtual Light* (1993). Stephenson presents Americans as in collective flight from the real America, seeking refuge in identical urban residential complexes. The only ones to keep in touch with America as it is are the street people 'feeding off debris'. Hiro is typical of these in manoeuvring his way through the rackets and negotiating his way through the virus which, as in William Burroughs, is a catch-all term covering computing, disease, and even language. Throughout the novel, Stephenson distinguishes VR from concrete reality, using the Street in much the same way as Gibson evoked the Sprawl, namely as a virtual highway peopled by countless 'avatars', another term which Stephenson appropriated from Hinduism to mean computerized versions of the self. In *Snow Crash*, avatars gather at a virtual nightclub called the Black Sun, a name suggesting an occult, secret interior, but in fact emerging simply as a conflation of real-world meeting places.

Scott Bukatman has argued that cyberpunk and other 'terminal identity fictions' offer the most reliable reports on contemporary culture by embodying the feel of the electronic systems which dominate the modern world. They offer visions of the post-mechanical, which is by definition the most difficult form of technology to visualize, and yet it is their strategies of visualization which link much contemporary SF film and fiction. In the last works discussed, the major single theme is one of connection so varied that the separation of the self from technology becomes impossible. The Australian SF writer Greg Egan has made the relation between electronic technology and human identity a central issue in his novels. *Permutation City* (1994), for example, depicts complex virtual-reality constructions and describes a process of 'copying' from human brains. Shelley Jackson has drawn on *Frankenstein* and the Oz stories for her electronic collage novel *Patchwork Girl*. And Mark Amerika created a 'virtual writing machine' in *GRAMMATRON* (1997). More recently, J. C. Hutchins's SF thriller about a secret government project, *7th Son* (2009), has been released as a podcast novel as well as in print form. Lastly, Geoff Ryman powerfully evokes the coming of information technology to a central Asian republic in *Air* (2004), whose title refers to a form of the Internet. The transformation of that culture is reflected in the gradual 'electrification' of the text which progressively includes more and more email messages and audio-file transcripts.

The perceived acceleration of technological change has resulted in the formulation of the concept of the Singularity primarily by the futurist Raymond Kurzweil and the SF author Vernor Vinge. Applying an evolutionary model of change, they predict a new era of superhuman or human/machine intelligence, which sounds millenarian in its optimism, spiritual in its promise of transcendence, and somewhat like a science fiction narrative in itself. This climax to technological development has already received SF treatment in Ken MacLeod's *Newton's Wake* (2004) and in Charles Stross's *Accelerando* (2005), among other novels.

Chapter 4
Utopias and dystopias

Darko Suvin has defined the literary utopia as a '*historically alternative* wishful construct' (his emphasis) which is closely related to science fiction as a kindred genre and which should be addressed as a verbal construction and not as some kind of transparent account of another place. His linking of utopias with SF is helpful since they constantly overlap and their separation has less to do with conceptual rigour than with academic reluctance to devote serious critical attention to science fiction, now happily a prejudice of the past. Suvin enumerates the general characteristics of utopias as including an isolated location, a panoramic sweep to its depiction, a formal system, and dramatic strategies conflicting with the reader's presumption of normality.

The term 'utopia' is a hybrid, as many critics have pointed out, meaning 'eu-topia' (good place) or 'ou-topia' (no place). The word entered the language in 1516 as the title of Thomas More's famous work describing an ideally ordered island state somewhere in the New World, that is, somewhere in that part of the world then being opened up to imperial trade and conquest. More sets a pattern for future utopian narratives in presenting it as a report from a traveller, Ralph Hythloday, who functions as the intermediary between the reader's familiar world and the new realm. More also demonstrated the liability of the utopian form, namely its tendency to exposition and the striving of the new society towards order.

This last is an ultimate goal rather than a fact in More's *Utopia*, since the state exists within a geographical context of war (POWs supply the state with many of their slaves) and contains crime and dissent. More opposed material and sexual desire beyond state limits and sets the death penalty only as a punishment for second-time adultery. One last external factor might be noted. At the time of writing *Utopia*, More was serving as an under-sheriff to the City of London, and London has served as a unique stimulus to British utopian writing in being an unplanned city growing by accretion. The resultant pollution and social inequality had reached crisis proportions by the late 19th century.

Especially in the 20th century, utopias have tended to be replaced with 'dystopias', a term suggesting a mis-functioning utopia. These might have a satirical dimension, as in the African American George Schuyler's *Black No More* (1931), in which a scientist discovers a way of altering skin pigmentation so as to make it impossible to distinguish between the black and white races. As the treatments multiply, American society begins to break down. Far from bringing liberation – one of the main purposes of utopias – the new science brings chaos.

Utopian elements became central to 18th-century writers such as Daniel Defoe, Jonathan Swift, Thomas Spence, and Robert Paltock; the latter's *Perkin Warbeck* (1751) was one of the first utopian novels to situate its other society within a hollow Earth. *Gulliver's Travels* (1726) is one of the most famous examples of this period to use the convention of fantastic voyages to other lands to examine human nature. Apart from the comparative discussions of institutions in Books 1 and 2 through dialogue – a crucial medium for utopias – the narrative actualizes metaphors of size and makes a complex interplay of perspectives. Lilliput impresses Gulliver initially as a utopian garden state, but the diminutive size of the Lilliputians feeds his assumption of superiority. In Brobdingnag, this is rudely reversed and Gulliver's stature is reduced to that of a plaything. The effect is as if Gulliver's vision has shifted in focus from distance to close-up. The changes in perspective and the many references to optical instruments all suggest that Gulliver's perception of the human body is dependent on maintaining a certain distance and therefore a certain delusion. Each book of *Gulliver's Travels* mounts different assaults on human pride, pride in experimentation in Book 3 and in being a superior species in Book 4, where reason separates from human resemblance. Estrangement has again and again been proposed as a defining characteristic of science fiction, and if this is so *Gulliver's Travels* meets this requirement directly in its complex shifts in perspective whereby Gulliver becomes more and more the victim, or 'gull', of his own experiences.

The golden age of utopias

From the late 19th century up to the outbreak of the First World War, over 200 utopias were published, the majority of which, with a few famous exceptions, are still unavailable to the general reader. The reasons for this surge in production must have included the rapid pace of technological change, the concentration in the USA of capital in a small number of private hands, and an intensifying debate about social justice. The strategies used to establish these narratives vary from work to work. Samuel Butler, for example, draws on the older tradition of territorial exploration to take his traveller into a world which bizarrely inverts many values of Victorian Britain. *Erewhon* (1872) describes a society in which it is a crime to fall ill and where machines have been abolished because humans feared they would take over. The Canadian James De Mille combines shipwreck with the found manuscript convention in his 1888 novel *A Strange Manuscript Found in a Copper Cylinder*, describing a world near the South Pole where gender equality has been achieved. Alfred D. Cridge takes us to another planet embodying the best of the Earth in *Utopia* (1884), whereas Henry Olerich presents his report on society through the eyes of a visitor from Mars in *A Cityless and Countryless World* (1893).

While the latter were celebratory, negative voices were heard. The American Anna Bowman Todd's *The Republic of the Future or, Socialism a Reality* (1887) purports to be a series of letters from a Swedish nobleman visiting the USA in the 21st century. Although he is impressed by his speedy journey under the Atlantic by way of pneumatic subway, reservations begin to appear about automation when he stays for days in a New York hotel without meeting a soul. But the main thing to strike him is the physical flattening out of the city into the 'very acme of dreariness', a physical correlate of the political equality enjoyed in the republic. Monotony is the main theme of Dodd's portrait, monotony of dress and monotony of life, since the state has taken over so many functions. This aroused no misgivings in the narrator of Edward Bellamy's famous utopian novel.

Looking Backward, 2000–1887 (1888) was one of the most widely read utopias of the late 19th century. Its readership extended worldwide and an unintended tribute was paid when Czarist Russia banned the volume. Bellamy helped trigger the utopias of William Morris and H. G. Wells, and played an important part in the rise of the Nationalist movement in the USA, which was devoted to nationalizing industry. Bellamy's volume also helped to popularize the 'sleeper wakes' convention of having the protagonist sink into a prolonged sleep long enough to take him into the utopian future. Bellamy uses Boston as his key location to demonstrate the coming of utopia in 2000. Julian West wakes to find a spacious, sanitized city of broad streets and open squares. Social conflict has disappeared, as has the profit motive, since all industry has been taken over by the state and the army embodies an ideal of social coherence and organization. Production and consumption still seem to be separate and, although Bellamy gestures towards more liberated roles for women, an emphasis on their 'beauty and grace' suggests his state is still androcentric. Most surprising of all is the transition from private to state capital in *Looking Backward* and in its 1897 sequel *Equality*, where the change seems to have come about by peaceful revolution. It is a millenarian transformation apparently independent of any deliberate human actions.

Nothing could contrast more starkly with Bellamy's evolutionary gradualism than Ignatius Donnelly's 1890 novel *Caesar's Column*, which describes a cataclysmic uprising of American workers against the rule of an industrial oligarchy, with massive loss of blood; or Jack London's *The Iron Heel* (1908), describing the seizure of power in America of a proto-fascist oligarchy (the eponymous Iron Heel) by the 1930s. *Looking Backward* was followed by a series of sequels and homage novels by Bellamy's contemporaries and his influence has continued, notably in the fiction of Mack Reynolds, who was an active member of the American Socialist Labor Party and who specialized in what he called 'social science fiction'. Through the 1970s, in response to Bellamy's two utopias, Reynolds produced a series of novels which express far stronger doubts about millenarian hopes. In *Commune 2000 AD* (1974), he shows mobile communities in flight from an over-regulated urban society; *Equality: In the Year 2000* (1977) surveys the different social and sexual failings of the 20th century; and in *Looking Backward, From the Year 2000* (1973), Julian West is told categorically: 'There is no such thing as Utopia [...] It's an unattainable goal. It recedes as you approach it.' Reynolds's scepticism increased as his series developed.

In his review of *Looking Backward*, William Morris took Bellamy severely to task for overstating the ease with which his utopia came into being without challenging the monopolies of his time, in short for idealizing the urban middle class and prolonging what Morris saw as the 'machine-life' of the cities under central state control. His own *News from Nowhere* (1892) is equally vulnerable to the charge of idealization, but this time to the medieval guild system. Morris's narrative has an immediate visual impact in that his own sleeper wakes to a London transformed. The image of the city has become beautified by the erasure of all traces of Victorian industry and its attendant smogs, and their replacement by small, brightly coloured buildings. When the sleeper William Guest notes in passing that the scene reminded him of an 'illuminated manuscript', the analogy gives us a clue to Morris's transformation which is essentially a return to a neo-medieval city, in other words to a pre-modern state. One sign of this return is that there is no longer a sharp distinction between city and country, and the suburbs of Morris's day are once again villages. *News from Nowhere* describes craft guilds, a communitarian society in which crime has died out (presumably because the profit motive is extinct), but where women have a familiar conservative role as child-bearers. Exposition of the new society to Guest takes place as he is guided round London and later as he takes an excursion up the Thames. One of the most crucial sections concerns the change by which society was transformed, a change tied partly to historical fact. At one point in London, Guest experiences what in film terms would be a 'dissolve' from the Trafalgar Square before his eyes and the same square in 1887, when it was the site of a pitched battle between demonstrating workers and the police and army. According to Morris's utopian history, this acts as the trigger to a general strike and then a major social revolution.

The Wellsian utopia

In his reflections on the First World War, *What is Coming?* (1916), Wells admits to a 'forecasting disposition'. His utopian speculations about the future take a variety of literary forms. The very title of *The World Set Free* (1914) announces its purpose, since Wells found the desire for emancipation a universal factor in literary utopias, although the means of bringing it about sounds startlingly modern. Here, atomic bombs are deployed to wipe out the last traces of narrow nationalism. They also wipe out large numbers of the citizens living in the poorer parts of European cities, but the end evidently justifies the means since atomic war ushers in a new era of enlightened world government. *Men Like Gods* (1923) takes a group of Englishmen to another planet where they encounter a world of their own possible future, in which class and government have disappeared. As the century progressed, Wells, like Aldous Huxley, came to associate the future of the world with that of the USA.

In *A Modern Utopia* (1905), Wells adopts a hybrid method combining narrative with theoretical discussion and even figures the work as a cinematic production. He uses two voices, but here again he breaks with the pattern of a companion functioning as stooge. From the Socratic dialogues onwards, the second speaker's role is to feed the expositor the relevant cues, but Wells's botanist is there as an actively oppositional voice to the narrator's lofty theorizing. His presence helps Wells to comment on the whole tradition of literary utopias, to admit their speculative dimension, and, most important of all, to recognize the lure of attempting to correct the perceived messiness of the world. He insists that the literary utopia should be 'kinetic' to match the continuous change of the modern era, applying Darwin's notion of evolution, which Wells rephrases here as a 'universal becoming'. It is easy for the modern reader, with the benefit of hindsight from the 1930s dictatorships, to identify the totalitarian implications of Wells's utopia. His Darwinian horror of overpopulation producing species conflict motivates a proposal to get rid of 'weaklings'. With amazing nonchalance, he writes that the state will dispose of all deformed children and, although there are prisons, dissidents will be sent into exile to a convenient island. Far from disappearing, nationalism will simply be extended globally so that London will become the centre of a worldwide empire. In considering the role of women, Wells remained an essentialist, continuing to privilege their function as child-bearers, and he is equally conservative over race, drawing on evolutionary theory to justify the superiority of whites.

Wells's transformation of London makes extensive use of glass, no doubt in reaction against Victorian brick. The Soviet writer Yevgeny Zamyatin makes this same material central to his OneState city in *We* (published in translation in 1924), set in the

26th century. However, here glass has a different, more ideological function than simply to allow more light to enter. Jeremy Bentham's 1785 plan for a model prison called a Panopticon (literally, 'all-seeing') was designed to maximize the ease with which the authorities could monitor the inmates visually. Observation confers control equally in Zamyatin's regime, where the citizens have become numbers within a state run on the lines of mathematics and ideal efficiency. Where Ford is the tutelary industrial 'god' presiding over *Brave New World*, Frederick Winslow Taylor, the American pioneer of scientific management, is the theorist celebrated throughout *We*. Within the mathematical symbolism of the novel, unity is an ideal of state coherence, hence the public importance of the event which begins the narrative, namely the completion of the spaceship INTEGRAL by the narrator D-503. All characters are identified through numbers, consistently so since their sole importance lies in their relation to the whole. Dissidence is represented through the splintering of the narrator's self-image, his dis-integration, a process which can only be reversed through the quasi-therapeutic process of an operation on his Centre of Fantasy, a process resembling a lobotomy.

Wells's most elaborate utopian study, *The Shape of Things to Come* (1933), presents its narrative as an edited record originally written by Dr Philip Raven. In it, he traces the development through the 20th century of social upheavals culminating in another world war, the collapse of European nationalism and emergence of the World State, the rapid development of means of communication, and the improvement of humanity's physical wellbeing. Along the way, Wells includes jibes against earlier utopians. Roosevelt II publishes a study called *Looking Forward* and Aldous Huxley is noted as 'one of the most brilliant of reactionary writers'. Once again, Wells is using a linear evolutionary model, but there is a striking mismatch between this development and the increasing number of gaps in Raven's manuscript. Book 4 ('The Modern State Militant') should form an upbeat account of the culmination of this evolution but is only an 'untidy mass of notes', as if Wells was beginning to have doubts about the continuity of his own narrative.

State control in *Brave New World* and other works

The 1930s saw the publication of a series of dystopias where the working of states was imagined which exploited the demand for orthodoxy to erase individuality. James O'Neill's grim *Land Under England* (1935) combines hollow Earth fantasy (surreal flora and fauna) with a dystopian parable on the 'mass-hysteria of the race' as the narrator calls it. Descending through a trapdoor in Hadrian's Wall, he finds himself in eerily silent underworld whose inhabitants communicate telepathically. He fears that he too will be 'absorbed', that is, assimilated into a collective mentality where his identity will be totally lost. The dark underground setting gives an appropriately nightmarish dimension to his experiences of the 'monstrous machine' of this state, a displaced simplified model of the totalitarian regimes of that decade.

O'Neill's portrayal of the group mentality was pursued in the direction of gender by Katherine Burdekin's *Swastika Night* (1937), which describes a Holy German Empire in its 7th century. She shrewdly demonstrates the collocation of mysticism and paganism which ritualizes a total suppression of women to the status of birth machines. State iconography plays its part in supporting this ideology which, as so often in these dystopias, suppresses history. One of the most powerful moments in the novel comes when a character gazes in astonishment at a photograph of Hitler, not only totally different from the blonde Aryan stereotype, but even talking to a girl! Hitler has become assimilated into an explicitly racist state.

Aldous Huxley's *Brave New World* (1932) was partly triggered by revulsion from Wells's utopias, especially *Men Like Gods* (1923), and partly by then current speculations on biological engineering. Following his visit to the USA in 1926, Huxley became convinced that the future of the USA was the future of the world, and in a sense his 1932 novel offers a vision of global Americanization starting with the London skyscraper on the opening page. The society of the novel is based on the application of streamlined mass-production methods which became known as Fordism, where quantity and efficiency of output were paramount, to the birth process, far less fantastic now in the light of cloning technology. By designating the human 'products' Alphas, Betas, and so on, Huxley evokes a society in which destiny is biologically determined and where society's standardization is reflected in their uniform dress and idiom. Strictly speaking, it is inconsistent for Huxley to retain names since they would be an anachronistic trace of individuality, but in fact he uses them to suggest the set of concerns converging in that society, from behaviourism to Marxism and industrialism. *Brave New World* works as a satirical dystopia by sexual inversion, where monogamy is reprehensible, and also by describing two worlds – the rationalized World State and the 'primitive' world of the Reservation – geometrically separated from each other, and then showing the leakage between these two realms through misfits from each side. Huxley describes a politically indifferent world where the population accepts its endless leisure through consumption of the drug soma, an ironic reformulation of Marx's proposition that religion is the 'opiate of the people'. Now the opiate has become the religion of the people.

By 1958, Huxley had become a permanent resident in the USA and chose to frame his survey of American culture published in that year as a return to his famous dystopia. *Brave New World Revisited* paints a sombre picture of the ways in which the imagined forms of 1932 were being realized in the 1950s. Huxley perceived a massive centralization of power which was threatening individual liberty. 'Modern technology has led to the concentration of economic and political power', he warned; and his book was designed to alert the public to the workings of these 'vast impersonal forces'. The culmination of these tendencies would come, he insists, in the following century, the era of World Controllers and the ultimate realization of *Brave New World*.

Without him realizing it, Huxley's 1958 volume gave a summary of some of the main dystopian features of post-war American science fiction. The dangers of overpopulation are addressed in Harry Harrison's *Make Room! Make Room!* (1966) which describes the New York of 1999 as crowded and subject to constant food shortages. What Huxley calls 'political merchandizing' had become the subject of Frederic Pohl and Cyril M. Kornbluth's 1953 novel *The Space Merchants*, depicting a future when big business has usurped the function of government and outer space has become commodified as potentially residential. Behind the façade of glossy advertising, the novel depicts the suppression of political dissent and the use of peon labour to produce synthetic foodstuffs. The workings of an industrial giant (modelled on General Motors) is central to Kurt Vonnegut's first novel *Player Piano* (1952), which shows how the ethos of the company functions as verbal extension of its production line. Vonnegut, who has acknowledged his debt to Huxley, describes a displacement of human activity by mechanisms (hence the title) but also a 'mechanization' of the characters, as they demonstrate social orthodoxy by parroting routine slogans to each other.

In *Brave New World Revisited*, Huxley expresses his deepest anxieties about public receptivity towards processes which were operating beneath the surface of society. His discussion of brainwashing, which would be later picked up by writers such as William Burroughs, Anthony Burgess, and Marge Piercy, focused on the worst example of a general problem: the proliferation of techniques of manipulation. In 1932, the media were shown to be a means of extended distraction, and it was this aspect which Ray Bradbury developed in *Fahrenheit 451* (1951), yet another dystopia of the period which owes a debt to *Brave New World*. In the latter, Huxley punctuates his text with literary allusions to remind the reader of the cultural past that has been lost. Since in Bradbury's dystopia books have become forbidden, there is a constant meta-reference throughout the novel to its status as a fictional text, but instead of reminding us of its fictiveness, these references situate the reader in a relation of disobedience towards the regime. It is a novel about a world where novels are banned, and this paradox invites complicity with the protagonist Montag even before his dissatisfaction comes to the surface. Through a series of identifications (book-bird-person), Bradbury identifies the fate of books with that of society as a whole. Extrapolating this single issue, he demonstrates how the suppression of books constitutes a suppression of dialogue and the replacement of social interaction with the media 'togetherness' of television soap operas. In Truffault's film adaptation, the television programme which Montag's wife watches religiously is presented as a multiply framed electronic space which she is invited to enter. In the novel, however, consumerism impels her to create a fantasy of enclosure by four-wall TV screens similar in effect to contemporary 360-degree film showings. In the last section of the novel, Montag's flight from suburbia and the bombed city, he enters a symbolic domain inhabited by the 'book people', who learn entire volumes, thereby literalizing the metaphor of the book as person.

Nineteen Eighty-Four and its legacy

The adjective 'Orwellian' has become a standard descriptor of totalitarian regimes which are characterized by rigid systems of enforcing state authority. In *Fahrenheit 451*, Montag combines the role of fireman – that is, janitor, since burning the books is 'cleaning up' – and policeman. The latter role with its black uniforms was emphasized in Truffault's film to trigger echoes of Nazism, although Bradbury wanted the book-burners to retain a composite, catch-all identity. Enforcement takes place against a background of comparative prosperity, whereas George Orwell's *Nineteen Eighty-Four* (1949) evokes the austerity of immediate post-war Britain under a brutal regime which combines echoes of the Nazis (Hate Week) and of Stalin's Russia in the state intelligence apparatus and the endless doctoring of official 'history'. Winston Smith, like Montag, is an operative within the state mechanism granted rare opportunities to see at first hand the destruction of factual evidence. Bradbury describes the television

12. Still from Michael Anderson's *1984* (1956)

as entertainment; Orwell concentrates on its use for control, since hidden cameras are everywhere, even in the countryside. He evokes a society whose members spy and report on each other, but even more disturbingly never know when they are being watched by Big Brother, the extrapolated image of this state surveillance.

Even in his diary, Smith records his own fate. The novel grimly confirms this inevitability when an electronic voice in the hide-away announces that they are under arrest. O'Brien announces to a horrified Smith that the elite of the party consist of the self-perpetuating 'priests of power', because they control the means of shaping thought and perception. Correcting Smith's attitude is an irresistible process without even the aim of converting him into a model citizen. At the end of the novel, we are told that he loves Big Brother, an ironic conclusion in itself, but one rendered all the bleaker by the suggestion from precedents that Smith will shortly disappear, and disappearance implies execution.

An extended tribute to Orwell was paid in Anthony Burgess's own dystopian novel *1985* (1976), which is introduced through a series of reflections on dystopias; it is interesting to see how Burgess situates himself in relation to the tradition. He discusses Orwell's debt to Zamyatin and his rejection of *Brave New World*, keeping the fate of freedom at the centre of the discussion. Gradually, Burgess's hostility towards behaviourism takes centre stage, towards the Soviet state's support of Pavlov, and towards the later writings of B. F. Skinner, whose treatment of human subjects is attacked in *A Clockwork Orange*. What Burgess could not have known at that time was that Skinner was a participant in MK-ULTRA, the covert CIA programme of mind control. On the other hand, he certainly did know Skinner's own utopian novel, *Walden Two* (1948), which explored techniques of behaviour modification.

A Clockwork Orange (1962) reflected public anxieties over juvenile delinquency and also incorporated into its narrative the then secret experiments which were being conducted into conditioning. The extraordinary language which Burgess used in the novel combined Russian (it is called 'Nadsat', i.e. 'teenage'), Americanisms, and Cockney slang. For this, Burgess, who had some connections with the intelligence community, received assistance from an ex-CIA officer with an Eastern European specialism. The novel is narrated by Alex, a streetwise gang leader, and falls into three phases: Alex's recreational violence leading up to his arrest; his imprisonment and rehabilitation therapy; and his return into society. To Burgess's annoyance, his American publisher initially dropped the final chapter, leaving Alex in limbo without a future. The use of Alex's voice for narration immediately situates us within the mentality of a subgroup with a casual attitude towards violence, sexual and otherwise. Hence the novel, and even more Kubrick's 1971 film adaptation, have been criticized for beautifying the actions of Alex's gang, but the novel's claim to be a dystopia actually lies in the description of Alex's treatment by aversion

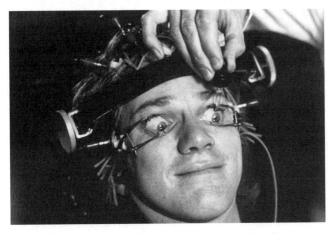

13. **Still from Stanley Kubrick's *A Clockwork Orange* (1971)**

therapy, a negative conditioning to link violence with nausea in his mind. This process, the substance of Book Two, is carried out through film viewings conducted while Alex's eyes are held open by an ophthalmic frame, one of the best-known images from the film.

Burgess consistently attacked B. F. Skinner, the leading proponent of behaviourism at the time, because he thought that treatments such as that endured by Alex removed the subject's volition. *A Clockwork Orange* could thus be read as an attack on official behaviour modification similar to Marge Piercy's *Woman on the Edge of Time* (1976), in which the protagonist is subjected to electro-convulsive therapy, or Thomas M. Disch's *Camp Concentration* (1982), in which the narrator unwittingly acts as a guinea-pig in a covert government experimental facility. All three novels are narrated by the subjects of these experiments, the status of whose subjectivity is left problematic by the very nature of their treatments.

The constructed worlds of Philip K. Dick

In contrast with utopias, which sometimes narrate their own construction, in other words their hopeful intentions, dystopias tend to be presented as already in place, and the narration usually follows that of a deconstruction of the existing regime through the actions of a protagonist who is a misfit, somehow skewed, like Montag, in his relation to the operative status quo. Philip K. Dick made this relation central to his fiction, in which he is constantly asking the question 'what is real?' This was partly a metaphysical issue for him, but also a problem of how to negotiate the projected realities of his time, since, as he himself explained:

> today we live in a society in which spurious realities are manufactured by the media, by governments, by corporations, by religious groups, political groups – and the electronic hardware exists by which to deliver these pseudoworlds right into the heads of the reader, the viewer, the listener.

Typically, Dick's protagonists exist embedded in complex and malign organizations, whose workings can scarcely be glimpsed, never mind understood. The recurring impulse in his works remains this drive to understand, despite the mystifications of the prevailing regimes.

Time Out of Joint (1959) remains one of Dick's most powerful explorations of institutionalized deception, in its description of the experiences of Ragle Gumm in a small American town of the period. Discrepancies in Gumm's reality mount, most dramatically with the disintegration of a soft-drink dispenser before his eyes. As he discovers more and more signs that he seems to be at the centre of a massive conspiracy, Gumm finds himself caught between a terrifying present and a bogus past, rival images of America closely connected with the fears of nuclear war prevalent at the time of writing. Gumm is the typical Dick protagonist in gradually discovering his entrapment by larger forces. Indeed, Dick's fiction grimly accumulates situations in which the protagonists find it impossible to verify their own identity. *The Penultimate Truth* (1964) depicts life in underground complexes where the inhabitants depend totally on the media for their information on the outside world. The 1966 story 'We Can Remember It for You Wholesale' (adapted into the 1990 film *Total Recall*) shows commercial and political systems of memory implant. Reality in Dick's fiction is always elsewhere, beyond the reach of his protagonists, and his darkest novels strategically confuse the reader so that we closely identify with these characters' paranoia. The most extreme treatment of this theme comes in *Lies, Inc.* (1966/1984) in which the protagonist fears that he is receiving subliminal messages from a giant computer corporation; and in *VALIS* (1981), Dick's last completed work, in which characters speculate on the nature of Earth as revealed through an extraterrestrial intelligence system.

Feminist utopias

Women writers have participated in the writing of utopian fiction from the very beginning. Margaret Cavendish's *The Burning World* (1666) is one of the earliest descriptions of a separate world, approached via the North Pole, where scientific enquiry is compared to the practices of contemporary England. Thanks to historical research by feminist scholars, which produced the Charlotte Perkins Gilman revival of the 1970s and the rediscovery of writers like Katherine Burdekin, we now have a much clearer sense of the contribution by women writers to the utopian and other traditions within science fiction.

Mary Griffith's *Three Hundred Years Hence* (1836) is the first American utopian novel to be written by a woman. It describes the experiences of a male time-traveller who falls asleep to awake in a future where railways have proliferated, transport has been revolutionized by self-propelled vehicles, and where the sexes have achieved equality. Whereas these utopias regularly examine the relation between the sexes, Mary E. Bradley Lane's *Mizora: A Prophecy* (1881) is unusual in describing a utopian world where men have disappeared completely. The novel is narrated by Vera, a Russian princess shipwrecked in the Arctic, who descends through a polar opening into a subterranean world. There, she discovers a society of women who have removed social conflict and produced a 'land of brain workers', where the physical body as well as the body politic have become subjected to rational scientific management. At the same time, God has become identified with the matrix of Nature, and when Vera gazes in awe at the panorama of Mizora without limits, the landscape embodies the women's confidence in their society. It is a world where commerce has become centralized and separated from profit, where electricity is widely used, and where science has become applied to every aspect of life. But it is a white world, a society of white buildings and white blonde women produced through the application of eugenics.

Charlotte Perkins Gilman's *Herland* (1915) gains much of its initial force from undermining the male pattern of lost-world narratives. Her use of four male protagonists suggests right from the start her avoidance of reductive stereotypes. Terry represents the crass adventurer, but Van the narrator is a much more judicious assessor of their experiences. Gilman humorously describes the disempowerment of the four travellers, who are treated kindly enough, but as babies. Though she does not avoid exposition completely, the novel dramatizes the exposure of gender prejudice through small details of style and dress, through what would be called in the 1960s the 'politics of behaviour'. In fact, by her questioning of presumptions of gender, Gilman shows a gradual estrangement of the narrator from his own masculinity and implies that gender is performative, more a matter of social conditioning than physiology, a position later theorized by Judith Butler.

During the 1970s, on the back of the civil rights movement of the previous decade, a renewed concern with gender showed itself in American science fiction, which in turn showed itself in the production of feminist utopian novels and also in the identification of a tradition of earlier fiction stretching back into the 19th century. Pamela Sargent's *Women of Wonder* anthologies restored attention to lost works like Francis Stevens's *The Heads of Cerberus* (1919), in which three characters are transported by means of a grey dust to the 'uncanny romance land' of a future Philadelphia. At the same time, a number of writers were directing polemic against the sexism of traditional SF writers like Heinlein, and of American society in general. One of the most complex figures in this area has been Alice B. Sheldon, the former CIA intelligence analyst, who published fiction under two pseudonyms, male (James Tiptree, Jr) and female (Raccoona Sheldon). In her story 'The Girl Who Was Plugged In', the female narrator challenges her male readership ('zombie', 'dad') to hear how she is offered a different physical persona by being connected electronically to a synthetic, nubile 'elf', an ironic parable about the male-centred social prescription of female beauty.

Joanna Russ has been one of the most trenchant critics in this field as well as one of the most innovative. In 1972, she declared that American literature 'is not about women. It is not about men and women equally. It is by and about men.' And in 1983 she published an ironic guide book entitled *How to Suppress Women's Writing*. Partly, Russ was clearing a space for her own fiction in these statements, but she was also challenging unconscious habits of taste and preference, challenging her readers to re-examine the depiction of women and outsiders in science fiction. She helped consolidate a view that women had been continuously suppressed in earlier science fiction. This position has become more difficult to maintain, as more and more earlier works of SF by women are rediscovered, and it has been criticized for historical distortion.

Russ's 1975 novel *The Female Man* contains four protagonists, all linked to the author by their initials: Joanna, living in present-day America, who feels that she has to masquerade as a 'female man' to negotiate through society; Janet Evason, from the utopian planet Whileaway, where men are extinct; Jeannine, a New York librarian living through an extended Depression; and Jael, an ethnologist assassin living in a world of overt war between the sexes, named after a biblical character who kills a Canaanite general. As happens in *Herland*, the four protagonists prevent any single female stereotype from emerging and embody different roles which interact within the novel: the social observer, the freed woman, the historian, and the militant. The novel constantly mixes its modes, jumping from interview transcript to first-person narration, as well as from protagonist to protagonist. Part Two opens with the question 'Who am I?', and the whole novel operates in the interrogative mode. It is sometimes unclear which 'I' is speaking, but that is strategic on Russ's part, since she constantly invites the reader to compare and contrast different episodes. At the conclusion, Russ revives the tradition of the 'envoy' to send her novel out into the society she is hoping to change.

The new feminist utopias tended to evoke female communities in which the birth process is managed by the women themselves, as in Suzy McKee Charnas's *Motherlines* (1978); or they presented conflict situations between the sexes, as in Sheri S. Tepper's *The Gate to Women's Country* (1989), in which a male warrior culture is contrasted with a separate women's world elsewhere.

A novel that sets up an extended dialogue between utopia and its opposite is Ursula Le Guin's *The Dispossessed* (1974), which opens with a Janus-image, the wall. The novel contains many allusions to the world politics of the time, when the Berlin Wall embodied the opposition between East and West, but Le Guin draws a further contrast between the material wealth and social conservatism of the planet Urras and the physical bleakness of the anarchistic utopian planet of Anarres. The novel was originally subtitled *An Ambiguous Utopia*, and Le Guin evokes this double perspective by alternating chapters located in each world. We are thus compelled by the very act of reading to cross and re-cross the 'wall' between the two. Shevek, the idealistic Anarresti protagonist, is skilfully used to encourage this constant comparing, especially when he visits Urras, since his outsider's perspective highlights the consumerism of this planet. He is also used more subtly to expose the covert ideological maintenance of orthodoxy in Anarres when his scientific research falls foul of the power structure which the planet's anarchistic claims deny even exists. The main city here is described as a model of utility, with its rectangular grid where nothing is hidden (supposedly), while on Urras Old Town is decaying and evocative of the similar district in *Nineteen Eighty-Four*, but still offers a kind of freedom. In an important essay, 'American SF and the Other' (1975), Le Guin has attacked the social conservatism of science fiction which 'has assumed a permanent hierarchy of superiors and inferiors, with rich, ambitious, aggressive males at the top, then a great gap, and then at the bottom the poor, the uneducated, the faceless masses, and all the women'. Russ would agree. She questions this division by bringing her extraterrestrial to New York, Le Guin by inducing a cultural relativism of perspective.

Where Le Guin shows utopia to be an ultimate goal unreached in her novel, *The Handmaid's Tale* (1985) describes a fundamentalist theocracy achieved. Margaret Atwood combines biblical allusion (her world is named Gilead), echoes of *Nineteen Eighty-Four*, and references to the evangelical Protestantism practised by part of the American Right to evoke another world where women have become reduced to physical facilities to serve the Guardians, the ruling male elite of this far from Platonic utopia. Atwood extrapolates familiar elements of 20th-century society to build up a misogynistic dictatorship, elements like the use of patronymics. The narrator is named Offred (i.e. Of-Fred) to suggest that she doesn't belong to herself. As a 'handmaid' – the term combines servitude with sexual exploitation – she has to service a Guardian regularly, which she manages by dissociating her mind completely from her lower body. Atwood suggests throughout the novel that Offred is someone else's, contained by a whole series of official interiors, a predicament which Offred endures by clinging on to increasingly tenuous memories of how things were 'before'. Unlike Orwell's protagonist, she possesses the narrative voice and therefore a symbolic self-empowerment within limits, since she can determine the shape her story will take. This perception offsets the bleakness of Atwood's vision of manipulation at all levels from brainwashing to sexual control, a theme developed further as bioengineering in her 2003 sequel *Oryx and Crake*.

Ecotopias and the *Mars* trilogy

In 1975, the novel was published which popularized and probably coined the term 'ecotopia', that is, an ecological utopia. Ernest Callenbach's *Ecotopia* is constructed as a series of reports by a journalist (William Weston) on a utopian enclave centring on San Francisco which has achieved independence for the USA. Weston records the transformation of living style which has been achieved through a return to some bucolic values and through a selective use of technology. Dress is simpler, pedestrians have a new priority in the city, and ritual war games are performed regularly to drain off aggression. As Callenbach admitted in retrospect, racial integration has not been achieved, however, and African Americans live on in separate areas known as Soul City. Nevertheless, his novel reflected a new environmental awareness which began to inform science fiction. Paul Theroux's 1986 novel *O-Zone* describes a future America where a huge part of the Midwest has been put in quarantine because of its pollution by toxic waste. Octavia Butler's *Parable* novels were fed by a concern over the inadequacy of food resources which brought about a collapse of civic society in California. *Parable of the Sower* (1993) describes the flight of a young African American woman north to found a community based on her religion of Earthseed, a kind of ecological vitalism. *Parable of the Talents* (1998) continues the narrative, but into a takeover of the community by religious fundamentalists.

The possibilities for action by the protagonists in the novels above remains limited by resistance from hostile groups or official inertia, but the main ecological utopia of the 1990s was Kim Stanley Robinson's *Mars* trilogy. This epic series combines utopia with the colonization of space, but Robinson has stressed that he did not want to present Mars as a refuge, more as a scientific and social laboratory. The volumes trace out a sequence of discovery and exploration starting in 2026 (*Red Mars*, 1992), terraforming the planet to make it habitable (*Green Mars*, 1993), and the extension of settlement and beginnings of fauna (*Blue Mars*, 1993). Mars itself is the true protagonist in this trilogy, with its own pre-human time of geological formation. Once the travellers from Earth arrive, utopia enters the narrative as a purpose and process. The first research station on the planet initially functions as a utopian site just as the novel creates sites for debate, but utopia also features as a holistic way of viewing the environment promoted by the American physicist Saxifrage Russell, one of the main

Utopias and dystopias

commentators in the novel. Robinson has stated that he wanted to move away from the older conception of utopias as separated places to a notion of them as a 'road of history', and throughout the novels he never lets the reader forget the trilogy's historical context.

How Mars has been imagined over the years is evoked through numerous allusions to Edgar Rice Burroughs, Arthur C. Clarke, and Alexander Bogdanov's *Red Star* (1908), an early socialist utopia set on Mars. Similarly, Robinson reminds us constantly of the economic cost of the expedition, supported by transnational corporations, and the persistence from Earth of ideological differences, which lead to a revolution at the end of the first volume. The many references to earlier SF writers in the trilogy in effect narrate the evolution of Robinson's own texts out of what could be called the 'Mars idea', and so the novels narrate two processes in tandem: the coming into being of a habitable Martian landscape and the formation of the novels themselves out of a matrix of utopian speculation. The subject of Mars continues to attract SF treatment because the wealth of information sent back from the landers still tantalizes writers with the possibility of life on that planet.

One last term should be noted here, one coined in the 1960s by Henri Foucault. The 'heterotopia' was used by him to contrast with the 'no-space' of utopias, in other words as an in-between, hybrid space which has an ambiguous status, possessing material actuality but also bringing complexity to location. This concept is particularly useful for applying to modern depictions of the city, as in Samuel Delany's *Dhalgren* (1975), where locales refuse to cohere, or in China Mieville's *The City and the City* (2009), where the reader moves between disparate spheres, sometimes distinct, sometimes overlapping.

Chapter 5
Fictions of time

More than any other literary mode, science fiction is closely associated with the future, in other words with time under its different aspects. It is above all a literature of change, and change by definition implies that the present is perceived in relation to perceptions of the past and expectations of the future which shape that present. Although speculations about the future had entered SF earlier through works like Samuel Madden's *Memoirs of the Twentieth Century* (1733) and Louis-Sebastien Mercier's *The Year 2440* (1771), a crucial catalyst to rethinking time was the formation of evolutionary theory in the mid-19th century by Charles Darwin and others. *The Origin of Species* (1859) and geological studies opened up the scale of time so that human history became merely a brief episode. On the other hand, Darwin's grand evolutionary narrative lent itself to contemporary race theory; the subtitle of *The Origin* was *The Preservation of Favoured Races in the Struggle for Life*. And its conclusion seemed to contain a message of hope: 'as natural selection works solely by and for the good of each being, all corporeal and mental endowments will tend to progress towards perfection'. Whether perfection is the goal or not, the very title of Edward Bulwer-Lytton's 1871 novel *The Coming Race* suggests that when the protagonist falls down a shaft to a subterranean world, he is encountering his own imminent future. Similarly, George Tomkyns Chesney's *The Battle of Dorking* (also 1871) had ushered in a new genre of future wars narratives in which territorial insecurities were given expression. Mark Twain's 1889 novel *A Connecticut Yankee in King Arthur's Court* could also be considered a story of time travel where a 19th-century Yankee, Hank Morgan, is knocked out and awakens in a medieval world. The time-travel strategy is used by Twain to set up a relentless satire of the whole Arthurian ethos, which is presented as pointlessly self-mystifying. Morgan here personifies a literal-minded practical intelligence which gradually demolishes the myths and ritualism of this other world.

In a 1902 lecture called 'The Discovery of the Future', H. G. Wells paid tribute to Darwin's study, explaining how it questioned the notion of a finite beginning and also questioned the finality of humanity. Accordingly, he concluded, 'we are at the beginning of the greatest change that humanity has ever undergone'. The optimism of this statement does not come out in Wells's 1895 novel *The Time Machine*, which is one of the formative narratives of time travel. In earlier fiction (and in later narratives, since the convention does not die out), the time traveller moves between periods by sinking into an unnatural sleep. Wells's novel marks an important departure from this practice in describing the transition as a mode of travel, and to do this he has to evoke time as space. Indeed, time is routinely evoked through spatial metaphors, and so time travel is simply making concrete tropes embedded in the language. The title of Wells's first attempt at time travel, 'The Chronic Argonauts' (1888), clarifies this strategy by suggesting that time can be traversed like a voyage, and *The Time Machine* depicts not only a vehicle but also describes the journey itself in terms anticipating those of an accelerated film, as happens in William Hope Hodgson's *The House on the Borderland* (1908). Wells saw himself as a secular prophet, educating his readership on the evolving tendencies within his culture, and the first section of his novel resembles a scientific lesson culminating in a demonstration. However, far from confirming any optimism about human evolution, the traveller's experiences disillusion him with progress when he encounters a world divided between the aristocratic and frail Eloi and the animal-like Morlocks who live underground. When he escapes from the latter and moves further forward in time, the experience is even bleaker. He finds himself on a beach, a threshold image, as if evolutionary beginnings and the imminent heat-death of the universe were converging in deepening darkness.

Wells's notion of a machine for travelling through time resurfaced in 1963 with the BBC television series *Doctor Who*, which used a (now extinct) blue police telephone box named the Tardis. Otherwise, time-travel narratives have tended to avoid physical devices. Jack Finney's *Time and Again* (1970) and its sequel *From Time to Time* (1995) describe how a secret government agency uses hypnotic techniques to regress characters back to earlier periods in New York history, the same process also being used in Richard Matheson's *Bid Time Return* (1975).

As time was opened up for multiple perspectives, the past as well as the future offered subjects for science fiction. This process was the central subject of Murray Leinster's 1934 novella *Sidewise in Time*, which presents an 'upheaval' in space–time. Strange discrepancies start appearing in the reality of a small American town, where Roman centurions are seen and at another point a sudden growth of primeval vegetation. The story is mainly focalized through James Minott, a maths instructor, who explains to his puzzled students that there are multiple futures and multiple pasts, linked by 'hyperspace', one of the earliest occurrences of this term in fiction. However, although Leinster attempts to juxtapose different period images, because the narrative is sequential, he can show only bizarre transitions. And because the 'time-faults' are presented through an analogy with earthquakes, his characters are helpless witnesses to a process which gradually stops of its own accord.

As a result of the post-Darwinian concept of time, a number of novels were published which present histories of the future. Olaf Stapledon combined within his *Last and First Men* (1930) Martian invasion and the exploration of the planets, but within a chronicle narrative stretching over a vast span of time. His narrator purports to be speaking to the reader from the far future and presenting the 'great theme of mind' which includes the serial evolution of different forms of humanity within a grand narrative designed to show how brief an individual life is and yet how large human potential might be. *Star Maker* (1937), published against the background of imminent war, builds on the subject of the earlier novel to describe the narrator's search for forms of intelligent life in the cosmos. The plot consists of a series of voyages through space without any technological underpinning, where flight is the physical counterpart of the outward reach of the narrator's mind.

On his journeys, he encounters different forms of life and different political organizations, which partly anticipate the themes of Isaac Asimov's *Foundation Trilogy* (later expanded to seven volumes) of the 1950s. This series was influenced in design by Gibbon's *Decline and Fall of the Roman Empire* and Arnold J. Toynbee's *A Study of History*. Set in a future where inter-planetary travel has become routine, the narratives are framed by entries from the *Encyclopedia Galactica*, a work of synthesis which exemplifies the working of 'psychohistory', devised by the founding sage Hari Seldon and defined as 'that branch of mathematics which deals with the reactions of human conglomerates to fixed social and economic stimuli'. In other words, it promises a large-scale system of predicting mass behaviour, not to be confused with the other 'psychohistory' which was also coined in the 1950s to describe the impact of striking individuals on history. Asimov's novels explore such issues as the relation of power centres to the periphery or of scientific advisers to political rulers, but only in the mass. Although he includes a character called the Mule who plays an important role in the break-up of the Galactic Empire, Asimov has no way of theorizing his role. The future histories of both Stapledon and Asimov had a strong influence on subsequent writers.

Prehistoric fiction

Once time was imagined as an expanse for exploration, the direction this could take was forwards or backwards. Narratives describing prehistoric beings have become known as 'prehistoric fiction', a phrase coined in the 1860s in France where this genre originated. Élie Berthet's three-part novel *The Pre-Historic World* (1876, translation 1879), for instance, opens with a description of Stone Age Paris, or rather the site of its future construction. The landscape contains no sign of human activity or construction, and thereby indicates some of the generic characteristics which came into operation. Because these novels describe a pre-literate world, we are unavoidably conscious on every page that the narratives are speculative constructs. Also they tend to be type-stories, showing general practices like species hierarchy or food-gathering. Prehistoric fiction offered a forum for discussing or giving physical form to evolutionary theory practised by a range of writers including Andrew Lang, Rudyard Kipling, and of course H. G. Wells ('A Story of the Stone Age', 1897). Lost-world narratives overlap into this genre since they regularly present accounts of exploration and discovery as journeys into earlier time. The guiding assumption behind Conan Doyle's *The Lost World* or the stories of Robert W. Chambers is that the primeval is physically accessible in the present, as if evolution were made up of a set of strands, each with its own pace.

One of the most famous early practitioners of prehistoric fiction was Jack London, whose *Before Adam* (1907) takes care to address the reader's scepticism from the very beginning. London's excursions into science fiction here and in *The Star Rover* (1914) are motivated by his impatience with mental limits. In the latter, his protagonist can travel at will into earlier periods. In *Before Adam*, the narrator describes himself as a dreamer who has the capacity to actualize any information he reads, rather similar to the opening of Michael Bishop's *No Enemy But Time* (1982), where the slide projections shown by the narrator's father act as a springboard for him to project himself back into an ancient African landscape. In *Before Adam*, this faculty is described as a 'race memory' which enables him to travel back to primeval time in order to experience the lives of his racial parents. His mother is 'like a large orangutan', his father 'half man, and half ape'. The novel thus explores a fantasy of heredity.

The sometimes awkward combination of contemporary narration with ancient subject is avoided by London in making his narrator a dreamer who takes the reader with him on his excursions, appropriately so since London wants to stress the continuity between the ancient past and the present. This awkwardness is also impressively avoided in William Golding's *The Inheritors* (1955), which skilfully constructs modes of utterance and perception closely geared to the capabilities of his Neanderthal subjects, who supply the perspectives for the early sections of the novel. Since 1980, one of the main practitioners of prehistoric fiction has been Jean M. Auel, whose series *Earth's Children* is set in prehistoric Europe. Stephen Baxter's 2002 novel *Evolution* sums up this Darwinian tradition with a sequence of narratives running from primates up to the present, each one adjusted to the perceptions presumed in each phase of development.

Future wars

Thanks to the pioneering research of I. F. Clarke, we now know what a large number of future wars narratives were produced especially in the period from 1871 up to the First World War, that is, during the heyday of empire. Although instances do occur earlier, the future wars subgenre dates from Chesney's *The Battle of Dorking*, which was published in the immediate aftermath of the Franco-Prussian War. This description of a German invasion of the British Home Counties was read in many countries, and it set a pattern for the works that followed in describing events happening in the imminent future when rapid changes in the political map of the world, mass communications, and military technology combined in narratives operating as national warnings about the need for preparedness. Future wars narratives connect closely with the practice of war gaming, which was introduced by the Prussians in the 1820s and which has since become institutionalized through computer simulations, sometimes so realistic that they become difficult to distinguish from reality. This difficulty, and the fear that the military might lose control of their own computer system, form the central subjects of the 1983 film *WarGames*.

Many future wars narratives from the turn of the 19th century are now forgotten, but in their time they dramatized the hopes and fears of empire. For instance, Louis Tracey's *An American Emperor* (1897) describes how a rich and enterprising American manoeuvres into the position of Emperor of France. More fantastically, Gustavus W. Pope's *Journey to Mars* (1894) recounts the voyage of American astronauts to the Red Planet, where they find a sophisticated race with advanced technology. They prove to be so friendly that the flagship of the Martian navy flies the stars and stripes in the visitors' honour!

The identity of the invader shifts from period to period. In Cleveland Moffett's *The Conquest of America* (1916), the Germans mount an invasion of the USA, whereas Frank R. Stockton's *The Great War Syndicate* (1889) shows war breaking out between the USA and Britain. These differences suggest the volatility of imperial politics around the turn of the century, but certain themes recur. American technical know-how and inventiveness is usually pitted against the more conservative military organizations of the European powers; and ultimate victory frequently goes to the 'Anglo-Saxons', that is, to an alliance between Britain and the USA. The racism implicit in many of these narratives became more overt in those dealing with the so-called Yellow Danger, which served as the title of M. P. Shiel's 1898 novel about a fiendish Chinese plan to take over the world. This they do by playing off the European powers against each other and, once they are weakened by war, the

Chinese launch an invasion of Europe. As they rampage through France, we are told that 'the bony visage of the yellow man, in moments of unbridled lust and mad excitement, is a brutal spectacle'. Defeat of the West is only staved off by spreading plague through the Chinese forces which wipes out millions, but which restores the ethnic status quo. Shiel's spectacle is no more lurid than the prediction of G. G. Rupert, an Oklahoma minister, in his *The Yellow Peril or, The Orient vs. the Occident* (1911) of a coming grand battle between armies of East and West when West will win, confirming biblical prophecies.

These future wars novels give us the relevant context for the most famous single invasion novel – H. G. Wells's *The War of the Worlds* (1898), which turns two images against the complacency of the period. In the opening lines of the novel, we are told that human specimens on Earth have been under observation from Mars as if they are of a lesser species. And secondly, when the Martians invade, their landing is directed against *the* imperial city – London. As a number of commentators have pointed out, Wells explicitly reverses the pattern of empire and reminds the reader to consider the fate of the Tasmanians – virtually extinct by the 1870s – as something that could happen to the British. The Martians are depicted as a double image, the one mechanical, the other biological. They prove to be indestructible by the main force of empire, the British navy, because they are easily mobile on land or sea and because they possess a deadly new weapon, their heat-ray. The original illustrations to Wells's novel repeatedly show skewed scenes, tilted at an angle as if to suggest the collective loss of balance in England.

Within their metal containers, the Martians resemble octopuses with large heads and atrophied limbs, which was the way Wells thought humanity would evolve. In that sense, *The War of the Worlds* shows humanity attacked by its own future. In George Pal's 1953 film adaptation, set mainly in California, the American army detonates an atomic bomb, which proves to be useless as defence against the Martians, and we shall see how the future wars

14. Original illustration to H. G. Wells's *The War of the Worlds* (1898)

subgenre was revived during the Cold War in descriptions of nuclear conflict.

Post-nuclear futures

Although H. G. Wells yet again played a formative role in describing the first atomic war in literature, the subject developed an obvious urgency during the Cold War and was treated in a whole range of novels from the 1950s to the 1980s. In Wells's *The World Set Free* (1914, US title *The Last War*), the very title hints that radium is associated with utopian hope, the hope specifically of humanity moving into a post-national phase when warfare has become a thing of the past. Ironically, the novel was published in the very year that the First World War broke out. The 1945 bombings of Hiroshima and Nagasaki suddenly transformed Wells's scenario into an imminent reality, symbolized in the Doomsday Clock set at minutes to midnight which has appeared since 1947 on the cover of every issue of the *Bulletin of the Atomic Scientists*. Suddenly, time took on a precious value as many novelists counted down their future holocaust minute by minute. As ballistic missiles replaced jet bombers, warning time reduced dramatically, so that Janet and Chris Morris's 1984 novel *The 40-Minute War* (triggered, unusually, by Islamic Jihadists) packs its main action into a time-span covering less than an hour. In some utopian novels, such as Suzy McKee Charnas's *Walk to the End of the World* (1974), nuclear war exists in the back-story as a convenience to explain the dissolution of conventional society.

In the vast majority of nuclear war novels, the antagonist is the Soviet Union and the war is described in reactive terms from the perspective of Americans on the ground, where survival of the nation as well as individuals becomes the paramount problem. Indeed, in a number of novels, like Cyril M. Kornbluth's *Not This August* (1955, UK title *Christmas Eve*) or Oliver Lange's *Vandenberg* (1971), the USA is described under Soviet occupation. Philip Wylie's *Tomorrow!* (1954) unusually describes the actual bombing of two Mid-Western cities, whose inhabitants have been debating the value of civil defence measures. Wylie uses shock tactics in his graphic images of casualties – a baby cut open by flying glass, a man walking on his shin bones after his feet have been sheared off – to try to startle his readers into an awareness of the need for defensive measures, although by 1963, when his second nuclear war novel (*Triumph*) was published, his confidence in civil defence seems to have collapsed. In this novel, there is no relief from a totally destructive holocaust.

Also from the early phase of nuclear fears, Judith Merril's *The Shadow on the Hearth* (1950) shows the dynamic efforts of a New York housewife to cope with a nuclear strike through appropriate practical measures. The nuclear war novel which has stayed consistently in print since its first publication is Pat Frank's *Alas, Babylon* (1959), whose action belongs within a similar self-help tradition to that of Merril. Here, nuclear war is viewed from the distant perspective of a small town in central Florida, and the action concerns attempts to maintain civic order in spite of the rise in looting and other crimes. Frank's sanitized version of nuclear attack contains many weaknesses which become more and more evident as the novel reaches its conclusion, in particular the dependence of any town for its foodstuffs, medicine, and power supply on urban centres which have been destroyed. The novel thus staves off an inevitable collapse which will happen beyond the final page.

Frank's quasi-realist method resembles the understated narrative of Nevil Shute's *On the Beach* (1957), which together with its 1959 film adaptation became the most controversial account in that period of nuclear war. Shute had originally planned a story of survival, but as he learned more about the movement of fallout, he changed the plot and produced an account in which no-one survived. The novel describes the remorseless drift of fallout into the southern hemisphere following World War III, in particular its arrival in Australia. The action divides between the Melbourne area, where characters struggle to accept their fate, ultimately taking suicide pills; and the voyage of a nuclear submarine to the USA and other areas to look for survivors. To Shute's surprise, the novel became a bestseller. Stanley Kramer's adaptation broke with the emerging pattern in the 1950s of showing nuclear danger sensationally through the monstrous. *The Beast from 20,000 Fathoms* (1953) depicts a creature thawed out from the Arctic ice

15. Still from Gordon Douglas's *Them!* (1954)

by a nuclear blast, while *Them!* (1954) shows ants hugely
magnified by the radiation from a nearby test site.

In contrast, Kramer simply shows the gradual cessation of ordinary
daily activity by his characters and studiously avoided any sign of
hope that might soften the film's impact. Because this ran directly

counter to the Eisenhower government's civil defence policy, the film was attacked for its defeatism. Despite the questionable nature of its scientific premises, the film remains one of the most thoughtful and austere treatments of the nuclear aftermath.

Nuclear war fiction has had to deal with a recurring problem of expression: how to describe the indescribable. Very few novels depict an actual nuclear strike. The norm has tended to be descriptions of its after-effects, some time in the distant future. All writers agree that such a war would create a massive rupture in society; some depict the result as a reversion to a pre-industrial, ruined world. In Aldous Huxley's *Ape and Essence* (1948), Kim Stanley Robinson's *The Wild Shore* (1984), and similar works, characters scavenge for valuable traces of the world that has been destroyed. In other narratives, like Alfred Coppel's *Dark December* (1960) or Whitley Strieber and James Kunetka's *Warday* (1984), the latter presented as journalistic reportage, the landscape itself has become shattered, divided into polluted and habitable segments, which need to be rediscovered by the protagonists. The general emphasis for self-evident reasons in this fiction on survival has been powerfully contrasted in James Morrow's *This Is the Way the World Ends* (1985), in which the protagonist is tried by those killed in a nuclear war for signing away their fates to the 'MAD Hatter', an absurdist conflation of Lewis Carroll's character and the strategic principle of Mutual Assured Destruction. Morrow planned this work as an anticipatory tribute to the victims of war.

Two acknowledged classics of nuclear war fiction deserve special mention. Walter M. Miller, Jr's *A Canticle for Leibowitz* (1959) uses a tripartite structure to present nuclear war as the culmination of a Western obsession with rational scientific enquiry. The novel displaces the history of the Judaeo-Christian tradition on to the American landscape and re-runs history up the 1950s. This entire sequence takes place after an earlier nuclear war – the Flame Deluge – which has obliterated literacy and produced countless deformed humans. Miller recapitulates the cultural history of the West, the (re)discovery of print, the resurgence of science, and the formation of the modern nation state. The culmination of the novel comes with the ultimate repetition, that of nuclear war which breaks out afresh between the superpowers. Miller depicts Western history as a scripted cycle which is doomed to repetition. Russell Hoban also uses his text as a palimpsest in *Riddley Walker* (1980), a post-nuclear Canterbury tale, where the eponymous narrator circles his way round to Canterbury instead of taking a linear route. Hoban evokes a neo-Iron Age culture where Riddley enacts his name, confronting riddles as he walks around the landscape. His language, that of the text itself, is a kind of mutated English containing double meanings like the conflation of the Adam story with the splitting of the atom in the following passage:

> Eusa wuz angre he wuz in rayj & he kep pulin on the Littl Man
> the Addoms owt strecht arms. The Little Man the Addom he begun
> tu cum a part he cryd [...] Owt uv they 2 peaces uv the Littl
> Shynin Man the Addom thayr cum shyningnes in wayvs in spredin
> circels.

The punning here presents the opening of the atom as an act of physical violence whose consequences radiate outwards in a ripple effect reminiscent of bird's-eye diagrams of blast radii.

Alternate histories

If the timescale of science fiction can extend backwards as well as forwards, it is no surprise that a genre should have started emerging at the end of the 19th century when writers speculated on alternative courses known history might have taken. An early collection of alternate histories was J. C. Squire's *If It Had Happened Otherwise* (1931), in which writers like Hilaire Belloc and G. K. Chesterton speculate about key events having different outcomes and consequences. The genre came into its own after the

Second World War, and that war, together with the persistence of the Byzantine or Roman empires and the American Civil War, have persisted as the most frequent subjects of this fiction. All these narratives exploit a point of divergence, a fork in the path of history which goes in a different direction; and this point usually occurs during a war or a finite event like a battle or the birth of an heir; in other words, at points when the alternate modelling of a narrative need not be too complex.

The purpose of alternate histories is frequently to open up speculations about the contemporary world, since they perform a retrospective time loop gradually converging on the reader's present. Eugene Byrne and Kim Robinson examine the demonizing of the political Left in their story collection *Back in the USSA* (1997), which shows the consequences of a Communist revolution in America. Philip Roth's *The Plot against America* (2004) has Lindbergh usurp Roosevelt for the US presidency to show the prevalence of anti-Semitism in that country. And Harry Turtledove (frequently described as the 'master of alternate history') and Bryce Zabel question the post-assassination idealization of Kennedy in their online novel called *Winter of Our Discontent* begun in 2007, which shows the president surviving the attempt on his life and subsequently undergoing a trial for corruption.

Two American novels remain acknowledged classics of alternate history. Ward Moore's *Bring the Jubilee* (1953) describes a USA as it might have developed after a Southern victory in the Civil War. The new present is one of economic depression, continuing racism despite the abolition of slavery, and a very limited development of technology. The narrator, Hodge, disorients the reader from the first page by declaring that he is writing his story in 1877 despite the presence of later events. The narrative works on one level as an unusual form of *Bildungsroman*, describing Hodge's experiences in the book trade and his career as an historian. The central subject is thus history itself and Hodge's desire to construct the 'whole picture', but Moore presents such a disorderly society as to preclude rational description and includes allusions to so many historical writers (Brooks Adams, Randolph Bourne, etc.) that the reader's expectations of a single historical narrative are increasingly thrown into doubt. Hodge joins a group including a scientist who has devised a time-travel machine, and Hodge is given the ultimate historian's dream of revisiting the past to verify his knowledge. In the Battle of Gettysburg, however, Hodge inadvertently causes the death of a Confederate officer, thereby altering the course of the battle and of history itself, and is unable to return to his present. The effect is a narrative counterpart of a scientific experiment where the observer interferes with the data, negating the results.

Influenced by *Bring the Jubilee*, Philip K. Dick's *The Man in the High Castle* (1962) describes the USA divided between the victorious Axis powers. The novel explores the ways in which American history has become commodified through mass-produced 'souvenirs', and complicates its account with a 'counter-factual' narrative, *The Grasshopper Lies Heavy*, which combines fact (the Axis powers lose the war) with fiction (there was no Pearl Harbor). Through this novel-within-a-novel, Dick completely destabilizes our sense of historical fact and suggests a re-run of European history in that the Nazis plan to manufacture an incident in the Rocky Mountains to justify them invading the Western states and seizing control from the Japanese. Both Moore's and Dick's novels gain much of their force from their sceptical attention to history as a narrative construct.

An off-shoot of alternate histories developed in the 1980s became known as 'steampunk', to describe its projection of a cyberpunk ethos back in time to the Victorian period. William Gibson and Bruce Sterling's *The Difference Engine* (1990), for example, describes the impact of Charles Babbage's early computer on society. Their point of divergence is this actual invention and the resultant changes in information technology in a novel which includes pastiche descriptions of 19th-century England and historical figures jostling fictional characters. In a more light-hearted vein, Paul Di Filippo confronts Victorian solemnity in his *Steampunk Trilogy* (1995), which sees Queen Victoria replaced by a clone with an aggressive sexual appetite and Emily Dickinson and Walt Whitman not only meet but throw decorum (and their clothes) to the winds in passionate sexual encounters.

Disasters

Disaster, apocalypse, and the end of the world have been staple themes in science fiction, all with their roots in antiquity. Similarly, the end of the race was well established by the 19th century as a literary subject, most famously in Jean-Baptiste Cousin de Grainville's *Le Dernier Homme* (*The Last Man*, 1805) and Mary Shelley's *The Last Man* (1826); in the latter, a plague is the agency of extinction. Even works like these, however, balance their speculation of endings with simultaneous hints that life will somehow go on. Endings are never final. Amid the welter of holocausts, nuclear and otherwise, which were published after 1945, there is usually an indication of a surviving remnant or a decisive re-assertion of normal order once the disaster has passed.

Two opposing views of disaster scenarios have been expressed by Susan Sontag and J. G. Ballard. For Sontag, surveying SF films from 1950 to 1965, disasters tended to be presented in predictable patterns and were powerful but inadequate images of current anxieties. Ballard, in contrast, has declared that the catastrophe story 'represents a constructive and positive act by the imagination, [...] an attempt to confront the terrifying void of a patently meaningless universe by challenging it at its own game'.

Disasters can be triggered ecologically or by an external force like a planetary collision, but in neither case can the human victims do much to protect themselves from these chance dangers.

In M. P. Shiel's *The Purple Cloud* (1901), an explorer returns from the Arctic to find all human life wiped out by a poisonous cloud. One of the grim appeals of disaster fiction is the spectacle of cities emptied of their normal life, and indeed one of the most vivid scenes in this novel shows the narrator wading through hundreds of corpses at the entrance to Paddington Station in London. The action really consists of an extended tour around the world where his initial impression of widespread death is confirmed again and again. The only event to offset his solitude is his discovery in Istanbul of a girl who somehow has managed to survive, and in this way Shiel can hint at a new beginning with this latter-day Adam and Eve.

Ward Moore's *Greener than You Think* (1947) ingeniously transforms grass into a threat through its sheer size and proliferation. A form of devil grass spreads gradually over the USA from Los Angeles and then outwards into the rest of the world. Moore concludes his novel with brief diary entries suggesting a countdown to an imminent end-point when the grass will have smothered everything. In contrast, George R. Stewarts's *Earth Abides* (1949) describes the consequences of a sudden pandemic which sweeps round the world. The ecologist narrator Isherwood, or Ish (echoing Ishi, the sole survivor of the Yahi tribe), journeys east from California to New York recording the gradual breakdown of civilization, but then the second half of the novel concerns the formation of a community of survivors. Although disasters are always described as actual events, their origin or meaning can be directly political. Charles Eric Maine's *The Tide Went Out* (1958), for example, traces the efforts of a journalist to uncover the shocking truth that nuclear tests have damaged the Earth's axis so badly that the world's temperature is rising rapidly. In John Christopher's *The World in Winter* (1962), however, a natural decline in solar radiation is ushering in a new Ice Age, which has the ironic effect of reversing the dependency of colonies on their colonial rulers.

The other main source of disaster is of a comet approaching Earth from outer space. One early example can be found in the French astronomer Camille Flammarion's *Omega: The Last Days of the World* (1894). The novel opens with a brief lesson in astronomy to set up its subject of inter-planetary collision, confirms the threat from a new comet with a warning message from Martian astronomers, and then evokes the spectacle of a dying Earth: 'the entire horizon was now illuminated by a ring of bluish flames surrounding the earth like the flames of a funeral pile'. In fact, disaster strikes, but this is not the end of the story. Flammarion expands his perspective to a transcendental point from which he can survey the whole of history and arrive at a moral that time has no beginning or end. Later versions of this subject stress survival. Kenneth Bulmer and Philip Wylie's *When Worlds Collide* (1933) offsets disaster with a spaceship (a latter-day ark) which transports a saving remnant to a hospitable planet, and in Larry Niven and Jerry Pournelle's 1977 novel *Lucifer's Hammer*, the approach of a comet brings widespread destruction to the USA, leaving survival finally problematic.

In *Lucifer's Hammer*, the action takes place mostly in Los Angeles, which must be the most frequently destroyed city in literary history. At different times, it has been H-bombed, burnt to the ground, flooded, subjected to electronic melt-down, or has simply slid into the ocean after a massive earthquake. It is no coincidence that these fates should happen to the movie capital of the USA, since disaster films have remained popular since their real emergence in the 1970s. *Earthquake* (1974) continued the local use of Los Angeles as the site of disaster. *Deep Impact* and *Armageddon* (both 1998) adapt the paradigm of the comet from outer space, both leading up to last-minute reprieves for the Earth. Inevitably, disaster films try to out-do each other in spectacular images of destruction, always showing the ultimate triumph of technology in saving a city or the world.

Although they appear to describe catastrophes, Ballard's first novels were designed as a trilogy revolving around time. *The Drowned World* (1962) describes the transformation of the London area after solar radiation melts the polar ice caps in the year 2145. In effect, tropical flora and fauna are bizarrely superimposed on London, which has not disappeared, only been submerged. The protagonist Kerans exists in a fluid present where his few memories of the old world are receding. The second volume of the trilogy, *The Burning World* (1964) / *The Drought* (1965), describes a desiccated landscape of the future, where sand is Ballard's central image with all its traditional associations with time. The concluding volume, *The Crystal World* (1966), uses crystallization to give surreal transformations of the present. Once again, Nature is usurped and the organic structures of the Cameroon jungle are given a brittle, jewel-like texture. Strictly speaking, this trilogy consists of post-disaster narratives presenting surreal versions of our known world. Ballard has many times acknowledged his debt to the Surrealists, particularly to their games with substance whereby solid objects melt and flow.

In Ballard's early fiction, the different dimensions to time, as duration, history, and so on, shift constantly, just as science fiction in general has repeatedly presented time as a spatial expanse which can be explored backwards into the past, into the future, or laterally into alternate histories. Many science fiction writers would agree with Samuel Delany's denial that they are dealing with the future, but that history in this fiction is actually giving 'distortions of the present'. In fact, time is a much more complex factor in SF and in our general culture. The Dutch writer Fred Polak's monumental study *The Image of the Future* (translation 1961) argues that the weakening of utopian hopes and eschatological faith has locked the modern age into an extended present, but the sheer vitality of the fiction discussed in this chapter suggests that the time-consciousness of SF continues to be a dynamic field of speculation.

Chapter 6
The field of science fiction

In this final chapter, I shall not be offering a definition of science fiction, but will be arguing that its repeated attempts to redefine or redescribe itself are integral to SF as it progressively tries to situate itself in the literary market place. In the introductory address to his 1894 novel *Journey to Mars*, Gustavus W. Pope addresses the problem of how to classify his narrative and attributes this difficulty to the rapid change of his age. One potential label for his novel could be 'scientific romance', a phrase which had earlier been used to describe Jules Verne's novels, but Pope notes that this had been attacked for the impracticability of subjects concerning inter-planetary travel, which to their critics were on the same level as the magical or mythic. Although Pope rejected this charge out of hand, it is a sign of science fiction taking on an identity of its own that he should introduce his first novel with a discussion of nomenclature. 'Romance' in 19th-century critical vocabulary was a catch-all term signifying a non-realist narrative. We thus have a tension in 'scientific romance' between the empirical and the extraordinary. In his 1933 preface to a collection of his science fiction, Wells returns to this question by drawing a firm contrast between his own works and those of Verne. The latter's extended detail has nothing to do with what Wells describes as his own 'fantasies', in which a single innovation is embedded in the 'commonplace world' for its consequences to be pursued. Wells's championing of the phrase 'scientific romances' is achieved by an extensive account of his own compositional practice, which he presents – again anticipating later discussion of SF – as aiming to set up new perspectives on human experience.

Media and intertexts

The urge to impose a single classification on SF ignores the generic hybridity of many novels: incorporation of the Gothic in *The Island of Dr Moreau*, of Shakespeare's *The Tempest* in *Forbidden Planet*, and so on. The rise of film coincides with the emergence of science fiction. The relation between SF fiction and film has included an ongoing fascination with spectacle and extraordinary special effects like those pioneered in Georges Melies's *A Trip to the Moon* (1902) and *The Impossible Voyage* (1904). H. G. Wells's own 'film story' *Things to Come* (1935) is one of the first screenplays published in book form and direct evidence of his participation in making a 'spectacular film' from one of his own works. In the period following the 1970s, Hollywood strengthened its dominance of SF cinema through its use of increasingly sophisticated special effects.

All texts are intertexts in that they generate their meaning with reference to other texts, but the intertextual dimension to SF is particularly strong, as a literary mode often finding expression in different media, especially the cinema. SF works are often not single but situated within a series. Take the following string of works from Wells's *The War of the Worlds* (1898). Within months of its appearance, a pirated version called 'Fighters from Mars: The War of the Worlds in and near Boston' had appeared in the *Boston Evening Post* (1898), transposing the setting and thereby facilitating subsequent adaptations. Also within the same year, Garrett P. Serviss redressed the Earth's defeat with his riposte *Edison's Invasion of Mars*. Here, the nations of the world under the leadership of the USA take the battle back to Mars and defeat the Martians (described as huge humanoids) at source. As the title suggests, Serviss's novel was a celebration of American military know-how, whereas the famous 1938 radio broadcast by Orson Welles and the Mercury Theatre represented an experiment in documentary techniques of reportage so convincing that the broadcast was widely taken as factual. In the post-war period, further variations on the story were woven by George Pal's 1953 movie, which yet again shifted the location to California and which showed the Martians to possess flying machines impervious even to atomic bombs. George H. Smith's *The Second War of the Worlds* (1976) addressed a similar threat, presenting a re-run of the action on a parallel Earth after the Martians have inoculated themselves against the viruses of the Earth. Despite this, they are still destroyed as they are trying to construct an atomic bomb. Finally, Stephen Spielberg's 2005 film takes the action back to the eastern seaboard of the USA, deploys more spectacular special effects, opens with the Martians already embedded in the ground, but re-cycles Wells's original ending of the Martians succumbing to infection. All of these works build significant variations on Wells's ground-text, adjusting it to different national urgencies or the possibilities of different media.

In the period since the 1970s, blockbuster films have produced different, more commercially motivated groupings of works. To take another famous example, the title of Ridley Scott's *Blade Runner* (1982) was taken from a William Burroughs screenplay-novel, which in turn had borrowed from Alan E. Nourse's *The Bladerunner* (1974), about smuggling illicit medical supplies. The action was adapted from Philip K. Dick's *Do Androids Dream of Electric Sheep?* (1968), which was then re-titled as a movie tie-in. The imagery of the film drew on *Metropolis* and film noir. The resulting film existed in different versions, notably international and US cuts. After the film's release, a number of film documentaries and book studies were published about the making of the film, which then found its expression in video games and continuations in three sequel novels by J. W. Jeter. By this point, it should be obvious that the main film represents an intersection point for multiple works before and after its release so diverse that the notion of a single, discrete work becomes an anachronism, replaced by a franchise or flexible commercial property.

Magazines and the science fiction community

The science fiction magazine has played a unique role in the development of this fiction, functioning partly as a medium for publication and partly as a forum for ongoing debate about the nature of this fiction. SF pieces were being published in a range of popular magazines by the 1890s, but the first SF-dedicated periodical was *Amazing Stories*, founded in 1926 by Hugo Gernsback. The opening issue identified a tradition by publishing tales by Poe, Verne, and Wells, who Gernsback situated within what he was now calling 'scientifiction', tales in which 'a charming romance intermingled with scientific fact and prophetic vision'. Gernsback saw himself as an educator, promoting science through this magazine as well as his other publications which included *Modern Electronics*. Accordingly, in this same editorial he insisted that the tales 'are always instructive'. Gernsback set the keynote for subsequent SF magazines by stressing the novelty of the fiction he was promoting and also by opening his pages to a running debate over the relation between science and adventure or literary interest in that fiction. During the 1930s and 1940s, the number of such magazines increased in the USA and Britain, and Gernsback's mantle as a shaper of science fiction passed on most famously to John W. Campbell, Jr.

Campbell took over the editorship of *Astounding Science Fiction* (later called *Analog Science Fiction and Fact*) in 1937 and rapidly transformed the journal into a medium for publishing rising young stars like Isaac Asimov and Robert Heinlein. Campbell's background was in technology, and in a 1946 editorial he declared that 'Science Fiction is written by technically minded people, about technically minded people, for the satisfaction of technically minded people', which sounds as if he shared Gernsback's preference for subjects. In reality, Campbell was far more varied and flexible about the fiction he accepted, and according to his authors his policy was far more important for its insistence on careful plotting, coherence of expression, and many other points which suggest that he was trying to inject a new professionalism into the writing of science fiction which was to pay off over the subsequent decades.

The magazines mentioned so far are American, but in the 1960s the situation changed with the appearance of a new publication. In 1964, Michael Moorcock took over the British journal *New Worlds* and transformed it into an important medium for experimentation in science fiction. In his first issue, he promised 'a new literature for the space age' and called for a revolution against the rather bland conventions of the 1950s. His policy involved cross-media attention, where graphics assumed a new importance, and his general assault on what he saw as a 'conspiracy of self-deceit' led him to champion controversial figures like William Burroughs and to participate in a broader series of challenges during the 1960s to taboos on expression and subject. Under Moorcock, *New Worlds* not only published a new generation of rising British writers like Brian Aldiss and J. G. Ballard, but also offset the American hegemony of SF magazines by attracting contributions from Thomas M. Disch, Thomas Pynchon, and others.

Apart from recognizing the role of science fiction magazines in the development of SF, we should also note the different ways in which the science fiction community consolidates its activities. In addition to literary magazines, fanzines (i.e. fan magazines, later known as 'zines') have played their part as amateur newsletters since the 1930s, often circulating news within a local SF society. In 1934, Gernsback founded the Science Fiction League, whose activities were taken over by the Los Angeles Science Fantasy Society in 1940. This was one of the earliest SF societies and numbered among its first members Ray Bradbury. A number of annual awards are presented by different SF associations, notably the Hugo (started 1955 and named after Gernsback), Nebula (since 1965 from the Science Fiction and Fantasy Writers of America), and the Arthur C. Clarke awards (since 1987 given mainly by the British Science Fiction Association and the Science Fiction Foundation).

Genre fluidity and generic reinvention

Science fiction is repeatedly linked with two proximate modes – the Gothic and fantasy. In his history of SF, Brian Aldiss takes *Frankenstein* as an ur-text, from which the two modes evolved in tandem. Fantasy, on the other hand, has been sharply distinguished from SF by some Marxist critics for consisting of narratives outside history, although critical writing on fantasy has often documented cases where SF shades into fantasy and vice versa within the same text. The British writer China Mieville has questioned this separation of modes within his own fiction and in his criticism, especially the notion that fantasy is anti-rational and dealing in impossibilities. He has argued that much so-called science in SF is 'point-and-wave' in that it presents only a semblance of scientific explanation, while fantasy can be responsive to analysis, declaring that 'the construction of a paranoid, impossible totality is at least potentially a subversive, radical act, in that it celebrates the most unique and human aspect of our consciousness'.

The promotion of SF at the expense of fantasy reflects a secularist ideology which has by no means been consistently central to science fiction. Turn-of-the-century narratives about Mars, for instance, repeatedly linked that planet with spiritualism. In 1903, the American naturalist Louis Pope Gratacap published *The Certainty of a Future Life in Mars*, which articulated a belief in a 'stream of transference', whereby life moves from one plane (and planet) to another. Here, Mars becomes a kind of utopian stopping-off point for the souls of the departed. More famously, C. S. Lewis's *Space Trilogy* appears to have shifted its emphasis towards Christian mythology during composition. The first volume, *Out of the Silent Planet* (1938), describes itself as a 'space-and-time story' explicitly acknowledging its debt to Wells; whereas the third volume, *That Hideous Strength* (1945), announces itself to the reader as a 'fairy-tale' inspired by Olaf Stapledon. Lewis is clearly not using this label in any negative sense, although the whole subject of religion in science fiction has tended to be neglected by critics at the expense of more materialist themes.

Nevertheless, religion has remained an important focus throughout the development of science fiction. Walter M. Miller, Jr's *A Canticle for Leibowitz* (1960) uses Christianity to mount an attack on the whole Western tradition of scientific reason which culminates in the production of nuclear weapons. And throughout his career Philip K. Dick describes attempts by his protagonists to transcend the material limitations of their situations and to find an ultimate truth. Frank Herbert's *Dune* (1965) is built around a symbolic linkage between the desert and Middle Eastern mysticism, though he makes little attempt to incorporate into its narrative the set of spiritual beliefs from which its appropriated Arabic terms spring. The astronomer Carl Sagan explored the difficulties of proving the existence of the deity in his 1985 novel *Contact*, and more recently Mary Doria Russell addressed the religious dimension to another alien encounter in *The Sparrow* (1996) and its sequel *Children of God* (1998). The presence of religion in science fiction is hardly surprising given its tendency to question limits and boundaries, and what could be more challenging than the limitation of mortality itself?

Apart from a recurring tension between spiritual and material themes, science fiction has become an increasingly hybrid entity. The 1960s saw the beginning of experimentation by science fiction authors with non-genre materials. The application by John Brunner of Dos Passos, by Thomas M. Disch of Dostoevsky and Mann, and later by John Sladek of 18th-century picaresque are only a few indicators of a general opening out of science fiction beyond its traditional generic boundaries.

Similarly, an important sign of the shift in the status of science fiction has been the increasing willingness of so-called mainstream authors to adopt its themes and practices. Billy Pilgrim, the protagonist of Kurt Vonnegut's *Slaughterhouse-Five* (1969), has come 'unstuck in time' as well as place, one sign of which is his transportation to the planet of Tralfamadore. Vonnegut draws on the SF tradition of extraterrestrials to suggest a mode of perception whereby everything exists simultaneously located on another planet because it cannot be found on Earth. By so doing, Vonnegut deprives any single narrative mode of an intrinsic authority, thereby anticipating Margaret Atwood's *The Blind Assassin* (2000), whose title actually identifies an SF story embedded within other realist narratives. Thomas Pynchon's *Against the Day* (2006) similarly contains a hollow Earth narrative of the kind popular at the turn of the century. What is happening here is more than a gesture to SF within individual works or an isolated excursion into SF such as John Updike's post-nuclear novel *Toward the End of Time* (1997), but a realignment of novelistic genres so that it is no longer assumed that science fiction is marginal. Doris Lessing made this point explicit in her preface to *Shikasta*, the first novel in her *Canopus in Argos* series (1979–83), when she declared that science fiction 'makes up the most original branch of literature now'. This process of mutual influence can be seen as a feedback loop between SF and non-genre fiction within a broader postmodern climate of breaking boundaries and protocols of expression. Pynchon's *Gravity's Rainbow* had a clear impact on cyberpunk writers; Kathy Acker then appropriated passages from *Neuromancer* for her own *Empire of the Senseless* (1988).

This cycle of borrowing suggests a constant willingness on SF writers' part to refresh their writings from diverse sources. Even L. Ron Hubbard, founder of Scientology and not a writer remembered for his experimentation, declared in his 1980 preface to *Battlefield Earth* that 'this is an age of mixed genres'. One sign of this desire for revision and refreshment can be found in the manifestos and packaging of recent science fiction. In 1983, the American mathematician and novelist Rudy Rucker published his 'Transrealist Manifesto' which made a plea for SF and fantasy reinvigorating realism. True to the political tradition of manifestos, it called for a revolution in representation which would break down consensus reality. Later in the same decade, when putting together *Semiotext(e) SF* (1989), Rucker and the other editors drew on the 'zines' then becoming popular in order to assemble instances of how the decorum of contemporary SF was being attacked or disrupted. The anthology includes graphics as well as poetry, diary narratives, a facetious style guide, a ribald version of *Frankenstein*, and many other pieces which demonstrate a collective wish to stand outside the mainstream of commercial science fiction. The editors present their contents as a harbinger of 'chaos SF', which is post-political and anarchistic.

Bruce Sterling's 1986 cyberpunk anthology *Mirrorshades* constituted a triumph of self-branding through a label which neatly combined information technology with popular culture and an anti-establishment dissidence. Even after the writers in that grouping had moved on, cyberpunk remained an important reference point for subsequent genres. Lawrence Person's 'Postcyberpunk Manifesto' of 1999 identified a shift, probably reflecting the age of the arbiters concerned, whereby protagonists were no longer solitary outsiders and where the societies described were no longer dystopias. A whole series of subgenres went spinning off from cyberpunk, including biopunk, consisting of narratives describing the totalitarian workings of business combines and engaging with the theme of genetic alteration not enhancement; splatterpunk, a 1980s coinage for a combination of graphic horror and cyberpunk; and steampunk, deliberately anachronistic projections of cyberpunk back into the previous century. The creation of these subgenres is a healthy sign of the collective self-examination and self-revision of SF by its practitioners. In 2002, Geoff Ryman published his 'Mundane Manifesto' which made out a case for moving away from space themes and the inherited improbabilities of inter-planetary travel in favour of a form of SF embedded in the subjects of Earth; in other words, a new form of social science fiction, which emerged originally in the 1950s.

Amid all this debate over the nature of science fiction, the African American voice has only become known collectively in recent years, despite the prominence in SF of figures such as Octavia Butler and Samuel Delany. In 1998, the Samuel Brandon Society was formed, named after a fictitious black fan writer, in order to promote ethnic science fiction. One of its founders was the Caribbean-born novelist Nalo Hopkinson, who has experimented with writing in Creole and incorporating Afro-Caribbean folkways into SF. Also in the 1990s, a looser movement came to be known as Afrofuturism, drawing some inspiration from cyberpunk SF. Despite its name, the polemicists of Afrofuturism deny that it is concerned with the future, but rather with reconciling black identities and the current technology of cyberspace. Because social estrangement is central to African American writing, and because those narratives tend to articulate a utopian desire for freedom, it is scarcely an exaggeration to argue that all African American writing is science fiction. A major promotional move has been made by Sheree R. Thomas's *Dark Matter* anthologies (2000 and 2004), which redress the perceived absence of African American writers from science fiction by collecting works stretching back to the 19th century and in the process demonstrating the actual existence of a neglected tradition. In his essay 'Black to the Future', collected in the first volume, Walter Mosley returns to a much-cited strength of science fiction as a 'literary genre made to rail against the status quo'. In making this claim, he is in effect joining the long line of SF writers who see that fiction as a unique medium of social analysis and challenge. These anthologies are performing a function in the USA similar to the broader purpose of Nalo Hopkinson and Uppinder Mehan's 2004 collection *So Long Been*

Dreaming, in which writers from former colonies confront their cultural inheritance through their attempts in science fiction to 'subvert received language and plots', as Mehan puts it in her afterword.

Science fiction criticism

We have seen how science fiction criticism originated within the mode itself because authors constantly debated the nature of their own fiction, and indeed SF writers have remained among the best critics in the field because every aspect is contested. Although there are isolated earlier instances, it was the 1950s that saw the emergence in the USA of science fiction criticism directed at a wider public readership. Contributing to a 1957 symposium on the social scope of science fiction, Cyril Kornbluth, a member of the left-wing Futurians group based in New York, attacked SF for failing to live up to its potential for 'effective' social criticism, arguing that it was compromised by Freudian symbolism. For him, 'effective' appears to mean directly altering social behaviour – a fantasy of literature's impact with a vengeance! But what is striking in his criticism is his assumption that science fiction should perform the function of social criticism. In fact, Kornbluth was being too harsh on the science fiction of the 1950s, which managed to escape the oppression of McCarthyism by presenting a mask of fantasy to the authorities. James Blish's satire on the period in *They Shall Have Stars* (1956), first in the *Cities in Flight* sequence, presents the USA as virtually a dictatorship. Publishing any novel in the 1950s which contained satirical portraits of J. Edgar Hoover as well as McCarthy was courageous, and Blish went on to publish important criticism under the name William Atheling, Jr.

The 1970s saw the emergence of academic science fiction criticism and increasing attacks on the parochialism of SF by writers like Stanisław Lem and Thomas M. Disch. Darko Suvin, co-founder of the journal *Science Fiction Studies*, presented the ground-breaking argument in 1979 that science fiction was the 'literature of cognitive estrangement'. His was a pioneering attempt to identify the distinctive practices of SF. The concept of estrangement is widely applied in literary criticism, but Suvin gives it a particular inflexion by insisting that science fiction texts are dominated by what he calls a 'novum' (a potentially awkward noun in implying reification or hypostatization of a concept), a term that can include a range of innovations from an invention to setting or a relation unfamiliar to the reader's worldview. Apart from his general insistence on the need for rigorous critical thinking about science fiction, Suvin's argument stressed the importance of perspective and the interplay between the reader's sense of the world and the different realities presented in SF works.

One last point should be noted about Suvin's critical writings. Without blurring the two areas together, he argues that science fiction and utopias are closely interrelated throughout their development and that the latter vary according to the historical urgencies of their periods. A similar linkage occurs in the writings of Fredric Jameson, another Marxist critic who has consistently linked science fiction to the larger socioeconomic processes at work. Jameson explains the contemporary age of postmodernism as one characterized by an aesthetic of depthlessness and of surface images or simulacra. His perception of the immersive nature of culture means that the critical reader has to become an 'archaeologist' in digging behind narratives to find further embedded narratives, hence the title of his major work on science fiction, *Archaeologies of the Future* (2005). Jameson constantly reminds us that expectations form part of every historical moment, and science fiction has a special role in articulating these hopes and fears, for instance in extrapolating a single perceived tendency into a dystopian future. China Mieville has drawn on the Marxist tradition of Suvin and others to re-socialize the concept of SF with its own protocols of expression and reception, and Carl Freedman has extended Suvin's analysis with his 'cognition effect'. If SF and fantasy are both attempting persuasion of the reader, the modes for him cannot be separated from each other or from history.

The Marxist line of SF criticism and its adaptations has proved to be the most productive, especially in its applications of the notion of estrangement. Feminist, poststructuralist, and queer criticism of science fiction has collectively unpicked the ways in which gender, identity, and sexuality have been expressed in ways which imply that certain structures are 'natural', especially in SF written prior to the 1960s. In that respect, the new modes of criticism are enacting the legacy of the surge of utopian, feminist, and anti-authoritarian movements of that decade. One of the most articulate critics of representing sexuality in SF is the African American novelist Samuel Delany, who approaches science fiction through its codes or cues to the reader. His own emphasis on the semiotics of SF texts represents a form of reader-response criticism closely tied to the details of verbal expression. Delany has described his continuing fascination with jewels as analogous to critical reading, in that they are beautiful objects but also a means of refracting light. Just as the jewels break up the spectrum, so Delany attempts in his critical writings to deconstruct SF prose.

It has been emphasized throughout this *Introduction* how close SF cinema is to SF fiction, although it has been argued that the former is essentially a post-Hiroshima phenomenon. Here again, applied Marxism has proved useful in articulating the nature of science fiction film representation: its privileging of image over dialogue, its anti-Faustian tendency, its shifting presentation of the alien, and its linkage between deep space and wonderment, among other themes explored by Vivian Sobchack, the leading theorist in this area. Since the 1970s, SF cinema has re-articulated our immersion in a depthless electronic culture. Since alienation is increasingly taken to be a condition of being, the very notion of the alien almost attenuates out of existence; our bodies and consciousness itself become technologized; and our sense of history becomes weakened. The result for film and fiction, it has been argued, is a tendency to pastiche (like the composite image of the Martians as robot-crabs in *War of the Worlds 2*, (2008)) and a more emotive exploitation of bigger and better special effects. Debate still continues on the question whether the collapse of generic boundaries in contemporary SF implies the collapse of textual meaning as tropes lose their traditional significance. However experimental an individual work might be, it will generate meaning partly through its interacting with the accretional 'mega-text' built up by science fiction over the decades.

Further reading

Introduction

John Clute and Peter Nicholls's *New Encyclopedia of Science Fiction* (London: Orbit, 1993) and John Clute's *Science Fiction: The Illustrated Encyclopedia* (London: Near Fine, 1995) are essential reference works. Three valuable histories of science fiction are Brian W. Aldiss and David Wingrove's *Trillion Year Spree* (Kelly Brook: House of Stratus, 2001); Edward James's *Science Fiction in the Twentieth Century* (Oxford: Oxford University Press, 1994); and Brian Stableford's *The Sociology of Science Fiction* (San Bernardino: Borgo Press, 2007). Among numerous other useful reference works are M. Keith Booker and Anne-Marie Thomas (eds.), *The Science Fiction Handbook* (Malden, MA, and Oxford: Wiley-Blackwell, 2009); Mark Bould et al. (eds.), *The Routledge Companion to Science Fiction* (London and New York: Routledge, 2009); Edward James and Farah Mendelson (eds.), *The Cambridge Companion to Science Fiction* (Cambridge: Cambridge University Press, 2003); and David Seed (ed.), *A Companion to Science Fiction* (Oxford: Blackwell, 2005). Joanna Russ's comments on science fiction can be found in *The Country You Have Never Seen* (Liverpool: Liverpool University Press, 2007). Istvan Csicsery-Ronay, *The Seven Beauties of Science Fiction* (Middletown, CT: Wesleyan University Press, 2008) presents a series of far-reaching essays on SF. Phil Hardy's *Overlook Film Encyclopedia* (New York: Overlook Press, 1995) is a valuable reference work.

Chapter 1

John Rieder, *Colonialism and the Emergence of Science Fiction* (Middletown, CT: Wesleyan University Press, 2009) explores the relation between science fiction and empire. Arthur C. Clarke's essays and reviews on science fiction are collected in *Greetings, Carbon-Based Bipeds!* (London: Voyager, 1999). A valuable source on *2001* is James Agel's *The Making of Kubrick's 2001* (New York: New American Library, 1970). J. G. Ballard's comments on inner space are collected in his *A User's Guide to the Millennium* (London: Flamingo, 1997).

Chapter 2

Useful commentary on the SF films of the 1950s can be found in Peter Biskind, *Seeing Is Believing: How Hollywood Taught Us to Stop Worrying and Love the Fifties* (New York: Henry Holt, 1983). Jenny Wolmark, *Aliens and Others* (Hemel Hempstead: Harvester Wheatsheaf, 1993) explores the relation of the alien to gender, as does Patricia Meltzer, *Alien Constructions* (Austin, TX: University of Texas Press, 2006). Gwyneth Jones's explanation of her Aleutians can be found in her *Deconstructing the Starships* (Liverpool: Liverpool University Press, 1999). Walter E. Meyer, *Aliens and Linguistics* (Athens, GA: University of Georgia Press, 1980) discusses the languages of different aliens in SF.

Chapter 3

Lewis Mumford's *Technics and Civilization* (1934) has been reprinted by Chicago University Press (2010). Graeme Gilloch, *Myth and Metropolis* (London: Polity Press, 1997) gives valuable commentary on Walter Benjamin and the city. Roger Luckhurst, *Science Fiction* (Cambridge: Polity Press, 2005) focuses its history on technology. Gary Westfahl, *The Mechanics of Wonder* (Liverpool: Liverpool University Press, 1998) discusses in detail Hugo Gernsback's role in the evolution of SF. Marc Angenot's introduction to the semiotics of SF can be found in his essay 'The Absent Paradigm', *Science Fiction Studies*, 6(1) (March 1979), pp. 9–19. Isaac Asimov, *Asimov on Science Fiction* (New York: Doubleday, 1981) collects essays on technology in SF and related topics. David Hartwell and Kathryn

Cramer (eds.), *The Ascent of Wonder* (London: Orbit, 1994) collects examples of hard science fiction, as does their subsequent volume, *The Hard SF Renaissance* (Pleasantville, NY: Dragon Press, 2002). Vivian Sobchack, *Screening Space*, 2nd edn. (New Brunswick: Rutgers University Press, 2001) gives essential commentary on relevant science fiction films. Chris Hables Gray (ed.), *The Cyborg Handbook* (New York and London: Routledge, 1995) contains many important pieces on this subject. Donna Haraway's famous 'A Cyborg Manifesto: Science, Technology, and Socialist-Feminism in the Late Twentieth Century' originally appeared in *Simians, Cyborgs and Women: The Reinvention of Nature* (London and New York: Routledge, 1991), pp. 149–81; it has subsequently appeared in numerous collections. Scott Bukatman, *Terminal Identity* (Durham, NC: Duke University Press, 1993) explores the emergence of the virtual subject in postmodernism. J. P. Telotte, *Replications* (Urbana, IL: University of Illinois Press, 1995) surveys robotics in the SF cinema, and David Porush, *The Soft Machine* (New York and London: Methuen, 1985) discusses a range of texts dealing with cybernetics. Mark Dery, *Escape Velocity* (London: Hodder and Stoughton, 1996) discusses the cyberculture of the late 20th century.

Chapter 4

Darko Suvin, *Positions and Presuppositions in Science Fiction* (London: Macmillan, 1988) contains his definition of utopias. His approach is followed in Tom Moylan, *Scraps of the Untainted Sky* (Boulder, CO: Westview Press, 2000). Krishan Kumar, *Utopia and Anti-Utopia in Modern Times* (Oxford: Blackwell, 1987) relates key modern utopias and dystopias to their political context. Philip E. Wegner, *Imaginary Communities* (Berkeley, CA: University of California Press, 2002) covers a much broader time span and also relates utopian writings to history. John Carey (ed.), *The Faber Book of Utopias* (London: Faber, 2000) gathers some classic examples of the genre. Pamela Sargent (ed.), *Women of Wonder: Science Fiction Stories by Women about Women* (New York: Random House, 1975), and *More Women of Wonder: Science Fiction Novelettes by Women about Women* (New York: Vintage, 1976) were pioneering anthologies in their field. Joanna Russ discusses the predicament of the female SF writer in *To Write Like a Woman*

(Bloomington, IN: Indiana University Press, 1995), and Ursula Le Guin's main comments on science fiction are collected in *The Language of the Night* (New York: Putnam, 1979). Eric Leif Davin, *Partners in Wonder* (Lanham, MD: Rowman and Littlefield, 2006) questions the received image of women's presence in science fiction 1926–65, arguing that it was far more extensive than widely supposed. Michel Foucault's 1967 paper 'Of Other Spaces' is available at <http://foucault.info/documents/heteroTopia/foucault.heteroTopia.en.html> (accessed 10 January 2011).

Chapter 5

H. G. Wells, *The Discovery of the Future* (London: Polytechnic of North London Press, 1989) reprints his famous essay. John Gosling, *Waging 'The War of the Worlds'* (Jefferson, NC: McFarland, 2009) discusses the radio adaptation of Wells's famous novel. Nicholas Ruddick, *The Fire in the Stone* (Middletown, CT: Wesleyan University Press, 2009) surveys the mainly Darwinian tradition of prehistoric fiction. I. F. Clarke, *Voices Prophesying War*, 2nd edn. (Oxford: Oxford University Press, 1992) gives an historical survey of future wars from 1763 to 3749. Related in subject, H. Bruce Franklin, *War Stars* (New York: Oxford University Press, 1988) examines the history of the super-weapon in American fiction. Paul Brians, *Nuclear Holocausts* (Kent, OH: Kent State University Press, 1987), with its 2008 edition at http://www.wsu.edu/~brians/nuclear/, are essential guides to fiction from 1895 onwards that deals with atomic war. Susan Sontag's essay 'The Imagination of Disaster' first appeared in *Against Interpretation* (New York: Farrar, Straus and Giroux, 1966) and has since been published in numerous collections. Samuel Delany, *Silent Interviews* and *The Jewel-Hinged Jaw*, revised edn. (Middletown, CT: Wesleyan University Press, 1994 and 2009) collect most of Delany's writings on SF. George E. Slusser and Colin Greenland (eds.), *Storm Warnings* (Carbondale, IL: Southern Illinois University Press, 1987) assembles essays on how SF confronts the future; and Fredric Jameson, *Archaeologies of the Future* (London and New York: Verso, 2005) presents a sophisticated Marxist interpretation of utopian and other SF. W. Warren Wagar, *Terminal Visions* (Bloomington, IN: Indiana University Press, 1982) is an important study of apocalyptic fiction.

Chapter 6

Mike Ashley, *The Time Machines*, *Transformations*, and *Gateways to Forever* (Liverpool: Liverpool University Press, 2000, 2005, and 2007) together make up the standard history of science fiction magazines. Michael Moorcock (ed.), *New Worlds: An Anthology* (London: Flamingo, 1983) gathers a cross-section of representative pieces from his journal. Mark Bould and China Mieville (eds.), *Red Planets* (London: Pluto Press, 2009) contains some of Mieville's statements on SF. Nalo Hopkinson and Uppinder Mehan (eds.), *So Long Been Dreaming* (Vancouver: Arsenal Pulp Press, 2004) is an important collection of postcolonial science fiction. Sheree R. Thomas and Martin Simmons's *Dark Matter* (New York: Time Warner, 2000) and Sheree R. Thomas's *Dark Matter: Reading the Bones* (New York: Time Warner, 2005) together constitute ground-breaking collections of African American science fiction. Studies of religion in SF include Frederick A. Kreuziger, *The Religion of Science Fiction* (Bowling Green, OH: Popular Press, 1982) and on its relation to philosophy, see Stephen R. L. Clark, *How To Live Forever* (London and New York: Routledge, 1995) and Susan Schneider (ed.), *Science Fiction and Philosophy* (Malden, MA, and Oxford: Wiley-Blackwell, 2009). Bruce Sterling (ed.), *Mirrorshades* (Westminster, MD: Arbor House, 1986) is the formative cyberpunk anthology. Darko Suvin, *Metamorphoses of Science Fiction* (New Haven, CT: Yale University Press, 1979) contains Suvin's classic formulations on this body of fiction. Patrick Parrinder (ed.), *Learning from Other Worlds* (Liverpool: Liverpool University Press, 2000) is a collection of critical essays on Suvin's writings. Carl Freedman, *Critical Theory and Science Fiction* (Middletown, CT: Wesleyan University Press, 2000) contains his discussion of the 'cognition effect'. The main critical journals on science fiction are *Science Fiction Studies* and *Extrapolation* in the USA, *Foundation: The International Review of Science Fiction* in Britain.

Index

ENGLISH LITERATURE
A Very Short Introduction
Jonathan Bate

Sweeping across two millennia and every literary genre,
acclaimed scholar and biographer Jonathan Bate provides a